Run, Witch, Run

Jonathan Grimm

Mountain Witch Press

Chapter 1

And therefore as a stranger give it welcome.

There are more things in heaven and earth, Horatio,

Than are dreamt of in your philosophy.

Shakespeare, Hamlet

Something stirred outside of Rachel's tent. *Have they found me? After all my precautions?*

She felt for the knife under her sleeping bag. It would be next to useless against creatures such as these, but she wasn't going down without a fight. *It was the channeling. If I hadn't used my Gift, they would not have been able to track me here.*

Where was Katie? Had they taken the little mountain witch?

Crack! A twig snapped outside. Rachel crawled closer to the tent flap, grateful she had surrounded her encampment with twigs and branches so as to give alarm should any creature – wild animal or hostile witch – approach.

1

Centimeter, by centimeter, avoiding any large or jerking movements, she pulled back the bottom of the left tent flap to peer out.

The moonlight backlit the trees, their irregular branches creating a saw-tooth pattern, and Rachel searched for movement among them. No creatures disturbed the stillness, aside from a hawk overhead, silhouetted against the dark sky, as it circled some distant peak. The breath of fresh, outdoor air, scented with evergreen from the pine needles that blanketed the ground, invigorated Rachel and helped her fight against the unconsciousness that threatened at any time to return her to the fever-racked stupor from which she had recently emerged.

She thought of backing up and cutting through the back of the tent, escaping before the creatures and their witch masters reached her, but days of illness had destroyed her strength. Rachel could not even sit up; her sweat drenched body was still under the covers – where she would likely die if she did not get help soon.

Overhead, an owl hooted. There was a stir of wings and the hooting stopped.

Another twig broke.

Would Katie come? Could she heal Rachel? Drive off her pursuers?

More twigs broke. Now, they were within feet of the tent. Rachel let the tent flap return to its place and opened her knife. The click of the locking mechanism as the blade snapped into place was like the crack of a hunting rifle in an isolated stretch of wilderness.

The sounds outside her tent ended abruptly; even the chirping of crickets ceased. Rachel clutched her knife and prepared to fight.

Chapter 2

Two Months Earlier

Apprehension roused Rachel from the borderlands between sleeping and waking. She had been conscious enough of the pitter-patter of rain outside her second story window, the whipping of the oak tree's limbs in the front yard, and the occasional rumble of distant thunder to feel the security of being indoors and protected from the storm yet still asleep enough to have the flood of recent troubles dulled – when she woke with a start. What if the noise of the wind and rain were masking the sounds of Katie outside, tapping on her window? If she were seen, both of them would be in danger.

She pushed off the covers, rose from her bed and walked towards the window. Turning her body at an angle so she would not be easily visible should someone be watching from the yard, she moved the curtain back a few inches. The rain and the darkness obscured her view, but when the lightning flashed, the roof outside the window became visible for an instant. No Katie. Rachel let the curtain fall back to its place but did not return to her bed.

Instead, she went to her bureau, opened the drawer and, forcing her hand to the very back, took out a traveler packet of tissues. Slipping her fingers inside, she felt for a bump among the soft tissues and removed the 27-carat, emerald-cut green amethyst gem she kept secreted there. She'd rather have a true emerald, but even this had been a financial stretch for her. The streetlights cast just enough light to reflect the stone's planes of brilliance. Rachel shifted it in her fingers, well satisfied that her study of physics allowed her to understand the principles of reflection and refraction that caused the gem to sparkle and separate the light into its component colors when looked through and moved just so. *At least my studies are progressing. Soon I will have enough knowledge to protect myself.*

In the narrow bookshelf at the back of the desk, stood the book on the magical world Katie, her mountain witch friend, had brought months ago as a gift. Rachel did not take it out; she had memorized it. Inside were woodcut illustrations of creatures such as mountain witches, miniature women who rarely exceeded three feet in height, yet were old in years and spoke with adult voice and language; human witches, sorcerers and sorceresses, and flora and fauna from worlds other than her own. There was also a section with beautiful, but forbidding, woodcut illustrations of less benign

5

creatures: ones that stole power from witches and others that took control of the bodies and minds of humans and animals. The book had a magic of its own and masked its contents to others by appearing as a thesaurus. It would even be a thesaurus for Rachel if she wished it to be – or needed it to be. Unfortunately, it was not an instruction book on magic. She really, really needed one of those, but how do you impress upon a mountain witch your desperate need for knowledge in the use of your gift? That your life could depend upon it because you were being stalked by those with the Power?

A tip, tap, tip on the windowpane broke her thoughts. Now that really was the little mountain witch. Rachel rushed to the window and pulled the curtains back far enough to see the round face of the tiny witch staring inside. Even with the familiarity that had come over the past months of their friendship, the witch's large blue eyes framed by a round, childlike face, still brought a smile to Rachel. She pushed the latch back on the window to let her in. Despite steady rainfall against the roof where Katie stood, no raindrops disturbed the witch's yellow, child's dress or the pink cloth hairband she wore in her smartly arranged blond hair. Were she not animated, she could have passed for a large doll, a two feet, seven inches high doll.

Possessing a nimbleness that had astonished Rachel when she first saw it, Katie climbed onto the windowsill and, in a jump, was through the narrow space Rachel had opened for her. The wind brought the smell of dampness and the wet and rotting leaves on the roof, but after she had closed the window, Rachel was met by the familiar and comforting scent of pine resin and dark, fertile earth that surrounded the little witch.

Katie bounded towards the bureau and Rachel knew she wanted her to take out the vintage mechanical watch she kept in her jewelry box next to a green marble Katie had left for her during a previous visit. Rachel obliged the witch and Katie wound the watch then held it to her ear and smiled as it ticked. Rachel wished she could have that childlike sense of wonder over something so ordinary as a decades-old men's watch with a cracked crystal and no band, but then remembered her own enchantment with the inexpensive gem she so prized - for the "green amethyst" was simply a piece of amethyst heat treated in the lab to turn it an artificial green.

"What a most singular thing this is!" Katie held the timepiece up to Rachel, speaking in a voice that was neither child nor quite adult.

"It's not even a good one. I got it out of an old, rusted coffee can filled with buttons and stuff I bought at the flea market for $2.00. If it were safe, I'd take you to a jewelry store and you could hold a real, fine one," Rachel said. She was grateful for the witch's ability to mask sound from leaving the room. That skill gave them greater security from discovery because Katie was always finding something that enchanted her or bouncing about, walking on the tops of the bookshelves as if they formed a sidewalk made especially for mountain witches to transit rooms upon. She could also speak directly into Rachel's mind, a sort of telepathy, but it so unnerved Rachel that she had finally had to ask Katie to stop doing so.

Katie jumped onto the bureau and returned the watch to its place, then rummaged through Rachel's CD collection. In between collections of Eastern European music, which her adoptive parents had bought her in better times, mistakenly thinking she would enjoy music from her native Romania, were more contemporary American titles. Katie grabbed one of these, removed it from its jewel case, pointed her index finger at it and it began to play REM's "Losing My Religion". This, using the Power to play a CD without a player, was a skill Rachel coveted, but hadn't mastered because she could not translate the CD's internal file format to audio as Katie could.

Was the mountain witch chiding her? Before it ended, Katie played a different tune: of the type popular with teenagers in the 1970's. Rachel didn't recognize it, and it certainly wasn't on any of her CD's so the witch must be able to store tunes in her mind, a sort of magical MP3 player. The miniature witch gyrated to the tune as if she were twirling an invisible hula hoop around her waist.

"Please, Katie, that's enough." Rachel laughed, despite her wish to be serious. "I can't take such upbeat music right now."

Katie didn't answer, but she did put the CD back in its case and selected another: "The Planets" by the Composer Gustav Holst, that Rachel had received as a gift from one of her mother's friends.

"How do you cloak the sound, again?" Rachel asked Katie as the music rose to a climax.

"Sounds are vibrations, so I create an opposing vibration that meets the first one when it exceeds the area I wish it to be heard. Like two tuning fork waves canceling each other out when the peak of one wave meets the trough of another, the second sound silences the first," Katie answered.

"It would come in handy for me to be able to move silently. They are getting more aggressive in following me. Tuesday on my school field trip to the Museum of Natural History, there was a woman. *I felt her.* She pretended to be asking directions of one of the museum staff, but I knew she was really just watching me."

"Just stay clear from them. Do not engage them in conversation and do NOT go with them. You feel them because you have the Power," Katie answered.

"But what do they want with me?"

"Do not worry about that."

"But I do worry, Katie!"

"I will not allow them to get close enough to you to harm you. Remember, the moment you first channeled the Power, I sensed it and was here the next morning. It took them more than two months to sense your channeling. I am more powerful than they."

Try as she might, Rachel was never able to get anything more out of Katie on the subject, and her circumspection and childlike figure with adult voice and diction infuriated, more than charmed Rachel, at such times.

The stairs outside her room creaked and Rachel froze. The footsteps continued onto the second floor hall and Rachel pushed her palms towards Katie to shoo the mountain witch away.

Katie smiled, as Rachel's pulse rose, but the little witch did not move.

The steps passed directly in front of Rachel's bedroom door but continued past, and Rachel sank back against her desk, allowing the tension to leave her body.

"Here, come sit with me." Rachel patted the bed beside her. "I need to know how to make fire without burning down everything around me." If the two of them were ever surprised by an unexpected intrusion, Katie could always scurry under the bed. Mountain witches could move with astonishing quickness, but, taking no chances, Rachel locked the door before walking to the bed.

Katie set the watch down and climbed into bed next to Rachel. When she was certain Rachel was paying full attention, Katie put up her finger and a luminous ball of blue light no larger than a BB floated out of it. Rachel started. "Don't catch the bed on fire, please!"

"Not to worry, it will not burn unless I wish it to."

"No, please, I don't wish it to."

"No, not the bed, the plasma. It will not leave its bubble and burn unless I will it to. It is trapped inside and has no oxygen to burn," Katie said.

"Here." Rachel leaned over the side of her bed, grabbed the small metal trashcan next to it and rummaged through it. She drew out a small plastic grocery bag, uncrumpled it, and put the waste in the bag with the exception of an old store receipt. Then she took the empty can with the receipt in it and put it next to Katie.

"Burn this, and let the ashes fall into the can," she told the witch.

Katie let the little ball of plasma float down upon the receipt. The girls nearly knocked their heads together peering into the can. The receipt didn't burn. Rachel looked at her.

11

"Now, watch this. I will release the flame." Katie stood on the bed directly over the pail. Like flash paper, the receipt was consumed in a burst of flame to gray, sulfurous dust. "Remember. There is more around you than you see. You are limited by your means of perception. Look…" She pointed to the electromagnetic spectrum illustrations in Rachel's book. "You cannot see this, yet it is. What your people cannot see or understand they call supernatural. That is a contradiction in terms. All things are natural; how could they not be?"

"Then what are you and I?" Rachel asked.

"We are creatures with extra senses. A bat has echolocation: which uses ultrasonic sounds to produce a mental image of its surroundings. An electric eel can produce hundreds of volts to shock its prey. You and I have extra senses that allow us to move things with our minds, transfer energy from one area and form to another, and see patterns where others don't – a heightened intuition, so to speak. That is our *Gift*. You try, now." She gestured towards the pail.

"No. Not in here. I could make a mistake. Even a small accident would lead to trouble for us. Later, out in the woods. I do really need to learn how to do this for when I flee –"

There was a sharp knock at the bedroom door and Rachel stopped in mid-motion of setting the can back in its place.

Chapter 3

Today Marks One Year Since Disappearance of Girls

Exactly a year ago today, the last of four missing girls, Kimberly Adams, a fifteen-year-old sophomore at Melville High School, vanished from her Melville home without a trace. Sources say police are looking for a suspect they have dubbed "ThinkingOfYou" after their online handle, and fear a serial killer may be at work in the Melville area. Residents worry police are withholding information from the public.

Detective Sergeant Candice Strong bristled at the last line in the *Melville Daily*. She, along with the rest of her department, was putting in sixteen-hour days on the case. She had worked into the wee hours and that was the reason for her late breakfast this morning. She contemplated reading the full article; although she knew she should take today off to recharge her batteries and enter the case fresh on Monday morning. She had on her tan running clothes. Candice selected the hot coffee, freshly squeezed orange juice, and blueberry muffin to give a burst of energy so she could burn off the tension of the case with a good jog around the park.

Instead, she picked up the phone and dialed the office. Detectives rotated Sunday shifts and her partner, Detective Charlie Webb, would be on duty this weekend.

"Mornin' sunshine," came Charlie's deep voice.

"Charlie, have you seen this morning's paper?" she asked.

"Yeah, can you believe it? Don't let it get to you, Candice. People are freaked out, right now."

"I know. That's why I moved to Melville from Chicago." She sighed. "Thought it would be quiet here and now we have kids disappearing without a trace."

No, not entirely without a trace - the fourth missing girl's computer was found still logged onto a social networking site. Kimberly, like at least one other of the other girls who were missing, had been corresponding with somebody.

"I just don't get this case. Most were isolated socially, had few friends, and either had trouble at home, school, or both. Yet, we don't have anything to suggest they were runaways," Charlie said.

"Yes, but who were they corresponding with? This town isn't big enough for four runaways not to be seen by somebody or picked up by police or social services at some point over the past year. Chicago, maybe. Melville? Just ain't happening, Charlie."

"Well, the FBI profilers have absolutely no idea what kind of perpetrator we're dealing with here. If we are even dealing with one."

"I'm dreading the meeting with them Monday morning. We don't have anything to give them and I'd stake my reputation that they don't have anything to give us," Candice said.

"Any idea of strategy?"

"We know that Kimberly went to the Melville river park on the night of her disappearance. Maybe we should sift through the evidence bags again. Possibly we missed something the times we scoured the area."

"It definitely wasn't in Kimberly's character to sneak out of the house at night. Her parents and classmates confirm this. She was a good kid. Got along with her parents. Just a bit of a loner."

"We do know she liked to go there in the afternoon to read and watch the boats sail up the river. Maybe that is where she met our Unknown Subject," Charlie said.

"Yes, but the only time the out-of-town girl, Esther Donalds, is known to have gone to the park was with her relatives, and her grandmother says she was never out of her sight."

"It is possible she ended up there or near there, at some point, and they just don't know. In any case, the park is the only physical location we have, so we'd better run with it," Candice said.

They continued to rehash the case and commiserate over the intense public pressure upon the Melville Police Department and Mayor's office to solve the case or, at least, have something concrete to tell the public. After hanging up, Candice retrieved her case notes from the study and flipped through them as she finished her, now-cold, breakfast.

Esther Donalds was only in the area to visit with relatives over the Easter Vacation. Both her cell phone and her aunt's computer were filled with text messages from "ThinkingOfYou". These texts were a bonanza for forensic investigators and the F.B.I. had attempted a profile largely based on the information found in Esther's accounts. However, there were too many anomalies to develop a consistent idea of the author. Even the world-class profilers of the F.B.I. had been stumped.

The youngest of the victims, twelve-year-old Jennifer Newell, had been heard by a neighbor conversing with an unknown woman a number of evenings, including the night of her disappearance. While it was possible there was no connection and Kimberly may have had her first, and only, meeting with the Unknown Subject the night she went missing, the consensus among investigators was that Jennifer had let the Unsub, or Unknown

Subject, into her house on several occasions while her parents were gone or sleeping. The girl did not have her own computer and her parents had restricted cell phone access to trips and other times when they needed to keep in contact.

Candice let the notebook fall back onto the table and pushed it away. The odds of these girls being found alive were slight at this point. Her mug was empty and she went to the machine to brew a fresh pot.

The warm coffee energized her and she went back to the notes on the Donalds girl. Try as they might, with all their combined resources and those of the FBI team, which an overwhelmed Melville Police Chief, under intense pressure from City Hall, had called in to help, they could not trace the person whose online handle was "ThinkingOfYou". This Unknown Subject puzzled investigators. Untraceable, and yet her writing was in many ways childish – or perhaps, just "childlike". Analysts could not determine whether it was an adult pretending to be a child or a child pretending to be an adult. Whoever she, or he, was, they were not comfortable with slang or current teen talk, yet, their texts and the questions they asked and the responses they gave to the missing girls, demonstrated a maturity – or cunning – that unnerved investigators. Right now, "ThinkingOfYou" was their strongest link, and best clue in the investigation.

Candice came to the last page of her notes. The final message on Kimberly's computer from "ThinkingOfYou" to the girl had been:

We'll meet at your favorite place. You will know me when you see me. I will be wearing a yellow dress.

Chapter 4

"**R**achel, are you up?" her mother asked from the hallway.

After hesitating a moment, Rachel replied, "Yes, I couldn't sleep." It must be later than she thought. She moved the physical science textbook she kept in front of the red LED of the alarm clock. 5:57 a.m.: the dark of the storm had masked the coming of morning.

"Good. I need you to get up and get ready for church. We have to leave early to pick up Uncle Joe. Your father will meet us at church."

Rachel turned to Katie, but the mountain witch was already gone. She was like that; she would come and go in an instant, without warning and without trace. Instead of looking for her or lingering on the visit, Rachel turned on the light and began to dress, glad she had showered before going to bed, because neither of her parents liked waiting on her.

The rain had subsided to a drizzle when Rachel and her mother got into the family's Subaru wagon. With all-wheel drive, her mother was able to drive slightly above the speed limit and maintain control on the water-slicked roadway. Rachel sat in the back so the front seat would be free for her uncle.

As they drove towards the exit of their gated community, Rachel scanned the area, searching for any trace of her stalkers: her ghosts, as she thought of them. If they were there, she did not see or sense them. She closed her eyes and relaxed back into the seat. It took some effort to avoid letting the Power channel through her and into her fingertips and lower extremities.

Her mother's silence, and the rhythm of the car wheels on the road as it passed over the bridge leading to the next town, where her uncle lived, lulled Rachel and she thought of how she had first discovered she had the Gift.

***

The night before the Fall Harvest Festival at church, she had a dream: of walking through the halls of her school, at a church social, then back at home. She was moving things with her mind, knowing other people's intentions even when they tried to hide them. The dream ended with her traveling to distant stars and worlds.

The dream had been so real, that, upon waking, she wasn't even sure it had even been a dream and not real life. Rachel walked around like a zombie for the week afterward. Finally, the feeling subsided and her life was returning to normal – when she had the dream again. This time she hadn't even remembered going to bed. She was walking through a hall, opening doors with her mind, searching for the right one. She didn't know what this right one would be, but felt she would know it when she saw it. While going through the hall, which was dimly lit, with only a single yellow light bulb above each door, she felt a presence behind her. She turned but there was nothing there. She woke and found she was sitting on the edge of her bed. Had she been sleepwalking? It was dark outside and, in a moment of panic, she began dressing for school. As she slipped on her skirt, she saw the clock on her dresser: it was 9:03 p.m. She sat back onto the bed to collect her thoughts. It was Friday night and she had no unfinished homework, and her parents were out visiting with church friends out of town and probably wouldn't be back until at least 11:00.

This had been so real, her ability to move objects, so true, that she could no longer dismiss it as a simple dream or nightmare. Something had happened to her.

The next afternoon in Algebra II class, as the teacher droned on about a formula Rachel had already committed to memory, her mind wandered and she decided to give these "powers" a try in the real world – if only to destroy the hold of the dream upon her by demonstrating its falseness. She looked at her pen sitting in the recess on the front of her desk and willed it to come to her. It immediately rolled to her hand. The motion had been so slight and subtle that, for a moment, Rachel doubted what she had seen. She placed the pen back in its groove at the top of the desk and tried again. It moved toward her the instant she thought come to me. Again she tried and again with the same result.

***

"Oh, no. The programs. We forgot the programs!" her mother said, jolting Rachel from her recollections.

"What programs?" Rachel tensed, sensing her mother was in a particularly sour mood this morning.

"What do you mean what programs? The ones for Wednesday's presentation. Didn't you see them on the counter?"

"No."

Janice Stephenson rapped the side of the steering wheel with the knife edge of her palm. "They were right there. You could have grabbed them. I had my hands full. Thanks a lot."

"I didn't know they were for church," Rachel answered.

"So you saw them but figured they just didn't concern you? What did you think they were for? Now I have to run them by during the week. Thanks a lot."

A number of responses ran through Rachel's mind, but it didn't matter whether she was guilty or not, and her parents had already taken her computer and cell phone; she didn't want to lose her precious physics books – not now – so she stifled a retort.

A few minutes later, they pulled up to Uncle Joe's house. Rachel started to rise from her seat to go knock on his door, but her mother interrupted her. "He sees us. Sit down."

Uncle Joe hurried through the rain, not quite running, but waddling, in his peculiar way. He was her mother's brother. His face showed a family resemblance, but he was heavyset, and unlike Rachel's father, didn't tuck in his shirt and rarely put much effort into fixing his hair. Yet, despite his unkempt appearance, he was well off financially due to his successful landscape contracting business and Rachel's parents often went to him for money.

"Rachel made brownies for our Potluck." Janice turned to Uncle Joe, after he put on his seat belt and settled in, and motioned, with her hand, to the glass pan in the back seat next to Rachel.

"Are you saying she actually stooped to cooking? What's next? Doing the laundry? Well, that was good of her. Are you trying to get money for new clothes, or something?" He asked with the sort of you can't fool me smile she was used to from him.

Rachel smiled to let him know he had an early victory in the chance that he would then leave her alone.

"Oh, goodie. Mind if I have one now?" he laughed. "Oh," he said as an afterthought and took out an envelope and handed it to her mother.

"Thanks." She quickly put it into her purse. "Don't just be a wallflower," her mother said to Rachel as they pulled into the church parking lot. "Try making some friends for a change. How's that for a unique idea?"

"I will," Rachel responded. Unlike the other kids, she had few real friends and belonged to no cliques. How could she tell her mother she simply didn't know what to say to them? That she tended towards the familiar and novel situations were difficult, and while she could handle simple conversations on set-up topics such as planning for a picnic or discussing a Bible passage, when left to her own devices, she faltered. But how could she tell her mother this when the woman would simply ridicule her and offer no help or suggestions, anyway?

"Sure you will." Her mother turned her face away from her, grabbed her books and church group study material, opened the door and got out. She walked away without another word or glance her daughter's way.

Chapter 5

A little philosophy inclineth man's mind to atheism, but depth in philosophy bringeth men's minds about to religion.

Francis Bacon

If that turns out to be true, I'll quit physics.

Max von Laue, Nobel Laureate 1914

(Speaking of de Broglie's thesis on electrons having wave properties)

Rachel grabbed her bible and put on her coat. The car was empty and she would walk alone to the high school group meeting room. She was careful not to trip as she made her way across the wet parking lot. She turned onto the walkway near the entrance and immediately felt the presence of one of *them.*

At the end of the lot, near the line of maple trees, stood a tall woman in a dark, antique style, blue dress with ruffled sleeves. She seemed to be waiting for someone. The woman did not glance at Rachel who lost her footing and skidded forward, barely keeping her feet on the wet pavement. Upon regaining her balance, Rachel made a hard right turn away from the lady, towards the church kiosk – and away from her destination of the meeting room.

The woman was of an indeterminate age; an age Rachel decided could be anywhere from the middle twenties to a graceful forty-five or even fifty. Such a broad range made her even more uneasy. Was this woman using the Power to mask her age? If so, why couldn't Rachel detect her channeling? Katie knew instantly whenever Rachel used the Power. How much more powerful and skilled was this witch? Was it even a witch or were her own fears causing her to imagine threats everywhere, even when none were present?

Rachel didn't look back as she passed into the church quad. The kiosk was in the corner and she lost herself in the crowd and took an alternate route towards Sunday school. The walkway was protected from the rain by a galvanized zinc canopy and Rachel glanced into each window as she passed, looking for any reflection of the woman.

Across the street, on the sidewalk in front of the homes, a man was walking his dog, a golden coated labrador on a chain leash. She sensed him before she saw him and knew at once that he was with the woman – another of her ghosts.

He had a rustic, athletic, hockey player, type look, but could also have passed for a high school biology or chemistry teacher of the sort who had come of age during the late 1960's or early 1970's and retained the New Age informality of that era. His jeans jacket was slightly out of style, but the dog looked like an expensive and well-groom purebred. Like the others, the man did not look her way even though she stopped and stared directly in his direction.

Rachel found herself behind the Johnsons as she made her way towards the high school group meeting room. Mr. Johnson waved in greeting while Mrs. Johnson, who was carrying her year old son Seth with one arm and holding the hand of Melissa, her four year old, with the other, smiled.

"Hello, Rachel," Melissa said. The girl was approximately the same size as Katie, but her childlike voice contrasted drastically with Katie's grown-up voice and college professor diction.

"Hello, Melissa." Rachel peered at Seth. "Good morning Seth."

The child didn't answer, but climbed further up his mother's shoulder. "He's tired," Mrs. Johnson said. "Oh, I meant to ask, do you think you will be free to sit for us on Friday?"

"I don't know why not," Rachel answered reflexively, then mentally kicked herself for committing to something she would be unable to follow through on. While she did not think those following her would harm the children, things had heated up to the point where she had to consider the possibility that she could be putting those around her in danger. She did like to babysit for the Johnson's, though. They represented the ideal family, even while she recognized that every family has its own set of problems.

"Thanks. I'll call you. Gotta go, love." Mrs. Johnson headed towards the nursery with her charges.

"Bye," Rachel said.

"Bye." Melissa waved with her free hand.

Rachel entered the high school group room with nearly half an hour remaining before the service would begin. Her friend Amy was in the alcove behind the stage in the front of the room, busy pulling puppets out of a large box with the rest of the drama team. Rachel decided not to go to her, for, while Amy was Rachel's best friend, Rachel was only one of Amy's.

The room doubled as both meeting hall and classroom for the Christian elementary school the church operated and, in addition to the stage in front, where church members performed Christian skits and music, the back half of the room had tracks upon which room dividers could be rolled out to form cubicles.

She went to the back of the room and set her Bible and jacket on one of the folding chairs set up for the service, but did not take her seat. Instead, she walked to one of the large windows on the side facing the parking lot. The woman was still there.

Rachel observed her as casually as possible without staring in her direction. This was the fourth definite time in the past few months that something like this had occurred. The first time, she had not seen anyone specifically, but while shopping in the mall felt a presence, as if someone, or something, was following, watching. Try as she might to dodge whatever, or whoever, it was, walking past a clothes store, then quickly ducking into it as she reached the end of its opening, using the clothes racks of designer jeans, kitschy t-shirts with captions such as "I'm With Stupid" as cover, making a large U-turn out of the other end of the store's front entrance, she had not lost her tail. There had been other times before when she had had the feeling of being observed, but this time she had been sure.

Rachel held her breath. If she were not so frightened by them, so new and unskilled in the use of the Power, she would confront this woman and demand to know why she was following her. The woman remained in place, as

31

if oblivious to Rachel's discovery of her. Rachel forced several long breaths in and out, and willed the tenseness from her body. Initiating hostilities with these beings, risking a fight she would almost certainly lose, would be foolish and her harsh early life had honed her survival instincts too keenly for her to try this. Her study of science, such as how to move a heavy weight with a lever, was only a workaround to compensate for her lack of knowledge, a lack this woman would not have – for Rachel was sure she was well trained in the use of all of her skills. Rachel sighed, this morning she had been certain her own study was teaching her enough to fight. Presented with the threat, in person, again, her confidence withered.

The service began. Rachel, who had moved to a seat closer to the window, channeled the Power. They already knew she was here, in this room, so channeling would not reveal anything they didn't already know. As the Power rose within her, warming and energizing her, she felt for the heightened intuition that came with it. Out of her peripheral vision, Rachel watched the figure for any change, but the woman in the parking lot remained fixed in her spot, without so much as a hand movement in response. When the Power reached its height, Rachel understood that they were watching her because she had the Power and would ultimately come for her and bring her into their world by any means necessary. Their world: one different and physically separate from Earth.

In the severely cut, velour dress, her light brown hair tightly braided in the Eastern European style, this woman was out of place, whereas the others had been dressed appropriately to a middle sized American town in Northern California. Was this one was of a higher rank than the others? What did they want with her Gift? To exploit it for their own ends? And what were those ends? That question, even magic assisted intuition would not answer. The day would come, and soon, when she would have to flee and hide and perhaps even to fight, prepared or not.

The first one had shown up barely two months after she first channeled the Power consciously, whereas Katie had shown up within a day. Were the two related? No, she did not think so. Katie had her issues, but she had never harmed Rachel, nor tried to frighten her, whereas, these were obviously silently stalking her – behavior that made Katie's circumspection seem like downright candor. Hence, she had begun studying science in earnest as a means of using the Power more efficiently.

She forced herself to ignore the being in the parking lot and think the problem through. They obviously knew where she lived, went to school and church, and could easily lay an ambush for her at any of these sites. Her long-term answer was to become proficient in her ability to defend herself. In the short term, however, she knew she could not either defeat them or, if she were honest with herself, even give them a real fight. No. She would have to flee.

The only plan she could think of was to cross the river and make for the hills and the dense mountain woodland that surrounded the town and continued nearly unobstructed to Canada. Toward this end, she had been collecting survival and camping gear and caching it in the hills behind her home. She did a mental inventory of her progress so far; a small two-person tent, hatchet, Swiss Army Knife, sleeping bag, a half-dozen lighters and two boxes of nutrition bars. The money she received babysitting was not nearly enough to finance this expedition, and this shortness of funds had hindered her progress. Nevertheless, she may have no choice but to flee immediately, prepared or not. Why wouldn't Katie help her?

The woman walked towards the building; her gaze encompassing the room. Rachel could now make out the antique style brooch on the dress. Was the dress really blue? Now it looked black. As the woman got closer, Rachel could see it was actually dark blue-green and glistening from her broach was an emerald, an emerald Rachel was certain was, unlike her own, genuine.

The skit ended. The students grabbed their chairs and carried them to the areas where each individual grade and sex met while the senior boys moved the dividers in place to create the temporary meeting rooms. Rachel was relieved; there were always specific themes and questions for the group to discuss. In an environment such as this, she thrived – and it would take her mind off of those following her.

"The verse for today is Romans 14:10. 'Why do you pass judgment on your brother? Or you, why do you despise your brother? For we will all stand before the judgment seat of God.' Does anyone want to begin?" asked Heidi, the college intern assigned to the eleventh grade girls.

Rachel considered the question. She liked and respected Heidi, who represented the best attributes of the Christian faith, while avoiding the type of spiritual one-upmanship, or concern with image and rules Rachel had seen in too many others. Though plump, the intern wore her weight well and her cheery manner was accented by the brightly colored homemade dresses she wore. Today, she was dressed in a pink skirt with lily patterns and a white blouse with embroidered collar that complemented it perfectly. On the back of her chair hung the blue, knitted sweater Rachel had so admired while Heidi was working on it during a church swimming party the summer before.

If there was ever a person she would confide in about her real stumbling blocks over the Christian faith it would be with Heidi. Damnation was Rachel's point of concern. How could God send the majority of his creation to eternal torture in hell simply because they were raised in a different religious tradition or could not see the Bible as the literal word of an infallible God? But she knew better than to ask this.

"Perhaps someone has thoughts on what this means and how to apply it to your daily life?" Heidi prodded when no one answered.

"It means not to be judgmental," Britney said.

"Good. In what ways?" Heidi asked.

"Not to feel superior to others and look down on them and like criticize them all the time and stuff," Teresa answered.

"I would also say, to not be legalistic," Rachel added.

"Legalistic. That's a good point. What do you mean by legalism, Rachel?" Heidi asked.

"Emphasizing rules and appearances and not acting with compassion and consideration to others. Looking only at those Bible verses that support their views or actions and not about their responsibility to others around them," Rachel answered.

"Now, that is an excellent comment, Rachel, Heidi said. "What do the rest of you think about that?"

The group discussion continued, but Rachel phased it out and concentrated upon her present peril. She had to strain her neck to see out the window inside their divider-created room. The woman was gone. Rachel couldn't be positive without getting up and looking out the window in all directions, but she no longer felt the woman's presence. It was as if the lady had wanted to be seen. Why?

Chapter 6

Rachel didn't linger in the high school room after the service but went directly to her parents' Sunday School Room. Usually, she waited and arrived only at the last moment, when her parents were preparing to leave, but today she felt safer around adults than alone in the church courtyard.

She could hear her mother talking as she entered. "It takes a lot of patience to be a parent. You have to set limits and enforce them. It's not always pleasant, but being a parent is ultimately about sacrifice. We chose to adopt an older child knowing the difficulties we would face. Jim and I feel God called us to this mission. Let me say, it has been more of a struggle than even we anticipated, but it has its rewards as well."

The divider was moved and Rachel strode forward wishing to appear as if she were walking into the room rather than having stood there, overhearing the conversation. Her mother's lips tightened but she remained controlled enough that only one skilled at reading people's gestures and body language as Rachel was, would catch the slight change. Mrs. Hennings smiled. There was an instant where Rachel saw one corner of the lady's mouth raising and contracting into an uncomfortable smile. Or perhaps a sneer? Whatever it was, it lasted only a microsecond, then Mrs. Hennings came forward and grabbed both of Rachel's arms in greeting.

"So how have you been, young lady? It is good to see you getting on so well. When you first arrived, you looked almost like a scarecrow!" She hugged Rachel.

Why did her parents gravitate towards ones like her, Rachel wondered, with so many good people to choose from? So long as they had their friends at church to sympathize with them and assure them of their rightness, nothing would change for Rachel. The Stephensons *had* been generous in taking her into their home, even if things had gone wrong the past two years.

A moment later, she caught her father talking to her mother privately.

"We'll just have to tell them we had a problem with the printer and will bring them later this afternoon." She knew her father was speaking about the programs, but was no longer surprised by his willingness to lie while considering it a grave offense in others.

Rachel was then irritated to hear several of the adults discussing their current favorite topic: the opening of a new Mormon temple in their area. She could not understand why they felt they had to denigrate the practices and beliefs of others so vehemently.

"They are growing. Each year there's more and more of them, you know?"

"Well, they do take care of their own. For all the wrong reasons, though—"

"Well, if by their works you shall know them...?" Rachel interrupted. "I mean, if they live clean lives, are good family people, and take care of their own, what is the problem with them? If you want to convert them just make sure your own lives are a model for others to follow. That would probably be a lot more effective as a witness than judgment would."

They looked at her like she had just thrown a water balloon at them.

"I think Rachel's just trying to cause a stir. She doesn't really believe this," her father said. He was wearing his dark blue business suit with light blue striped shirt and red tie. His hair was perfectly done, and his wire frame glasses gave him the air of a schoolmaster, while dress and manner would allow him to pass for a senior executive at a Fortune 500 company. Yet, in spite of his expensive clothes – and he spared little expense in dressing well – they were often broke.

Mrs. Hennings mumbled something about the Mormons going to Hell for rejecting Christ and moved away.

"Could I speak to you for a minute?" her father asked her when they had a moment of relative privacy, speaking in the tone he used in public to mask his irritation.

Once inside the room, he was at her in two long strides and hit her as hard as he could across the behind. The blow pushed her forward and she almost collided with the side of one of the cabinets. In the whispered growl he saved for times he wanted to yell at her, but could not for fear of being overheard by people whose favorable opinion of him mattered, he said, "Here," and handed her the car keys. "Go to the car and stay in it until we're ready to leave. Don't you dare let me catch you out of it. Your mother and I are both getting tired of your attention-seeking antics."

Rachel strolled across the parking lot, but turned towards the other side of the lot from where her family's car was parked. She couldn't see the woman, but this time she did feel she was being watched. Not from the parking lot, but elsewhere. Possibly from one of the houses across the street or one of the businesses further down the road. Wherever the woman was, Rachel was certain she could see her. She no longer sensed the presence of the man walking his dog.

41

Was this the time to run? She was not fully prepared, but she couldn't take any more of this cat and mouse game with her "ghosts" – and they were getting bolder each time. Plus, there was the deteriorating relationship with her parents to consider, the constant air of disapproval, of failing in some way, of being blemished, flawed. This did her far more harm than being struck. In Romania, she had been beaten near to the point of death. Her pain threshold was far higher than the Stephensons were able or willing to go – but their authoritarianism, control for control's sake, was driving her off. This controlling behavior was selfishness in her view, a willingness to hurt others in order to maintain a sense of control over their environment.

She would go. Just do it. The corner at the end of the street from the church had a stop for Bus 16 which went to within half a mile of her home.

As she walked along the sidewalk, towards the bus stop, she looked from side to side as unobtrusively as possible to see if the woman in the blue dress was in sight. Rachel did not see her, but she felt, if not the woman, then, something, behind her. By what mechanism were they following her? If she could sense them, she was certain they could sense her. But from what distance could they do so? Best to stick with the plan – get home and prepare to run. Worrying about them taking her at home would not help. In truth, they could seize her anywhere, once they made the decision to do so.

The offices on Rachel's side of the road ended, and the final stretch was lined with bushes. Behind them, several construction projects were in progress, but being Sunday, there were no workers to provide witnesses that might make these people reluctant to act here. She picked up her pace. It would be safer to wait at the bus stop than to linger in this vacant portion of the road. The main street diverged from the sidewalk and the sounds of the traffic were reduced here. To her side, Rachel heard some creature scurrying. Perhaps field mice, or even a cat, but when a gap opened in the bushes, she jumped backwards. A low riding creature, similar in size to a badger, with brown, matted fur, a beige snout and large paws, was staring at her. It took only a second for it to register where she had seen such a creature before – in "Powers of the Realm": the book Katie had brought her. It was a Possessor – a creature with the ability to take control of a person's mind.

Chapter 7

Security is mostly a superstition. It does not exist in nature, nor do the children of men as a whole experience it. Avoiding danger is no safer in the long run than outright exposure. Life is either a daring adventure, or nothing.

Helen Keller

Rachel ran as fast as she could, while mentally running through her small arsenal of defensive tactics. If there were sufficient moisture in the air around her, she could heat it and send it to the creature. Latent heat of vaporization was one of the first principles she had taught herself. But that would take time and would work better in ambush. Her ambush, though, not one she was caught in as here. So this is how they would take her: have a Possessor control her mind and lead her body to them? She picked up speed. The brush ended and she passed into an empty field where the sidewalk ended. She made a split second decision and cut across the field. There was another bus stop further up its route she could take once she had lost her tail. If she had lost it.

From behind, she heard a shriek, as of a wild animal wounded. The shriek was followed by screeching and growling – a fight of some sort. Had a dog attacked the Possessor? She didn't dare look behind, and continued her sprint into the neighborhood behind the field. From there she would intercept the bus a mile ahead at the other stop.

The creature wasn't following, or if it was, had some way of becoming invisible to her. Invisible or well camouflaged – she didn't dare channel to find out – that drew Possessors. She was confident enough to risk a bus ride. Her gut told her something had happened to it, that something had taken it out. What? Why? The magical world was full of predators – and prey – and her own knowledge of it was limited to what she had read in her one book.

The bus was stopped at the light ahead and Rachel hurried to get to the stop before the bus passed it. She made it and was the only person boarding at that stop. The bus was a dull steel color. The exhaust smell was very strong until she got up the steps, paid her fare and the driver closed the door. Less than half a dozen people were aboard and she felt no threat or attention from anyone. Good; fewer witnesses to her path as a runaway. A bald man with glasses looked up as she passed in the aisle, but she didn't think he was with those people.

So was it really time to flee? She considered this again
while the landscape shot by as the bus made its way
down the street. She certainly had been struck before
and no hits she had received here were even close to
what she had taken from complete strangers as an
orphan in Romania and those people, who she now
thought of as the Blue Dress People, they could follow
her anywhere, couldn't they? Her channeling must have
attracted their attention, summoned them, as it had
Katie. But if she didn't channel, and they didn't know
where she had fled to, could she be safe from them?
What about her parents? They could be difficult, but
they also had their kind moments. Life at their home was
better than anything she had had in Eastern Europe and
leaving to go live in the woods had no endgame. What
would she do in the long run? Maybe if she were picked
up after some time, her family situation would be better
when she returned. She had really been Mrs.
Stephenson's project; Mr. Stephenson was simply
backing his wife's wishes by supporting her parenthood
venture. One thing Rachel recognized – her adoptive
mother was more interested in having been a mother
than in actually being one – to have bragging rights, so to
speak. The first year had been great, but after the novelty
faded and parenting became real work, her mother was
onto other projects and hobbies and seemed to resent, at
times, her daughter's very presence. It was not too late
for Rachel to return to the parking lot before her father

found out she had disobeyed his orders to wait in their car.

No. She would leave. The encounter with the Possessor changed everything. She could not wait in place for these creatures to take her at their leisure. Rachel had lived on the streets before, and she could do so again, and fleeing would give her breathing space to teach herself enough from her science books to fight back against the forces arrayed against her. She did have some skills, acquired from her study of science and conversations with Katie, but she had been overconfident about her ability to use her techniques in the heat of battle, or, in this case, chase. Practice and increased knowledge would be in order.

Rachel forced herself to walk, unhurried, from the bus stop. As she turned onto her street, she saw the man again walking his dog on the other side of the road, a few houses down from hers. They had to know she had fled the church, but would they guess, or discern by the Power's intuition, that she was preparing to run?

Chapter 8

Rachel scanned the area around her home before going inside. Across the street, the neighbor's garage door was open, and their nephew was working on his car, music playing from a boombox on the shelf. Only his feet were visible as he labored underneath. Next door, the elderly Mrs. Norris was working in her kitchen. Neither saw Rachel approach.

She did not see anything lurking for her, and, for the first time since encountering the Possessor, felt relatively safe. Inside, the house was still – a stillness accentuated by the fact that nobody was supposed to be in there at this hour on a Sunday. She grabbed a box of crackers and pushed it into a garbage bag then took an empty plastic milk jug from the trash, washed it and filled it with water. This she put inside the garbage bag as well in case someone saw her leaving the house. No need to send up a signal flag saying "I'm going camping. Want to find me? Go look in the woods."

She hesitated at the kitchen table and thought of writing a letter to the police telling them she was a runaway who left of her own free will and not a victim of kidnap or murder. That would be the right thing to do. Also, if she were captured and returned home, she didn't want to risk any real future abduction being seen as her running away again. She paused, then put her father's car keys on the table. She could write a note later.

After packing some final food items, she ran upstairs. She couldn't forget the hairbrush. It lay on her dresser: a broad handled antique hairbrush. The brass was faded and needed polishing, with many of the bristles missing or bent, but to Rachel it was priceless. It had come from Meg, the elderly angel at the orphanage, who had befriended Rachel, then adopted her and brought her to the United States. But Meg was dead. Rachel had returned home from school one day in sixth grade to find she was an orphan again.

Meg had been a member of the same church as the Stephensons and they were one of the families who had opened up their home to Rachel after Meg's fatal heart attack. The Stephensons, who were childless, kept her the longest and her tenure at their home had eventually become permanent. Was she being ungrateful in leaving them? Mrs. Stephenson had stayed up with her on nights when she was ill and Mr. Stephenson used to stop by the bookstore after work and buy books for her.

Rachel held the brush for a few moments, then put it in her bag. Staying could put them in danger, couldn't it? If she was worried about babysitting for the Johnsons while being stalked, shouldn't she be even more concerned over her parents safety? Or was this simply an excuse to rationalize her leaving? The Blue Dress People had a definite agenda, but Rachel had yet to sense malice from them – even when channeling the Power she had not felt this from them.

She grabbed a pinecone she had collected in the woods and set it in the corner of the windowsill where it might serve as a clue to Katie that she had gone to the woods. The cone was dry and no longer smelled as strongly of the forest as it had when Rachel had brought it home the year before.

It was too late to return to the church with her absence undiscovered. There would be a lot of trouble from her father over that. Still, avoiding punishment was not a good reason to make such a monumental decision as fleeing.

If she went into the woods, she could study around the clock. Who knew what techniques she could learn, what new abilities she could discover? Maybe when she returned, the Stephensons would care more for her and things would go back to the way they had been during her first year with them. And she had tipped her hand to the people following her, hadn't she? Stick to the plan. She had been preparing for this day for a long time.

Before leaving her room, Rachel looked around one last time, then grabbed the nearly two hundred dollars of babysitting money she kept tucked under the desk calendar on her bureau and went to get her bike. Inside the garage were several cardboard boxes of old clothes and linen. She removed a small blanket from one and put it into her bag.

Rather than opening the front garage door and pedaling out, Rachel walked the bike into the backyard and took the gate on the other side of the house. It was obscured by bushes and this would allow her to get a running start before anyone walking on the street could see her.

After closing the gate behind, she put her knapsack down and leaned the bike against the side of the house. The music from across the street was still audible as she crept to the edge of the bushes. The young man across the street was still under his car, but she could not see Mrs. Norris. Rachel waited a few minutes, but Mrs. Norris didn't appear at any of her windows.

Rachel returned to her bike, hefted the pack onto her shoulders, checked to see her bag of water and food was securely attached to the basket behind the seat, and mounted. She pedaled down the Stephenson lawn and onto the empty sidewalk.

The woman in the dark blue-green dress was in the park as she rode up, as was the man, again walking the same golden labrador. Okay, this wasn't any different than dodging the police in Italy, who would return her to the orphanages in Romania, or the sex traffickers in both countries, sex traffickers in whose custody she would suffer a fate worse than the eventual death that would come in their hands, either by violence, forced drugs, HIV, or some other disease that a captive, weakened by malnutrition and abuse, would surely suffer from. Calm, she counseled herself, you can ride your bicycle through and use the parking lot and pedestrian bridge as a choke point. She would ride by, then turn at the last minute.

From the other side of the bridge, she could see the man on the path ascending towards the levee road. Rachel pedaled faster and continued as fast as she could until he was out of sight. She crossed at the footbridge that twisted around the park and crossed to the other side of the river. She continued along the bike path at top speed until she was too exhausted to continue.

When she came to a copse of trees, she rode into it. There was a large oak in the center; it shielded her from view. The wind was blowing, and drops of water from the rain earlier fell upon Rachel as the branches were disturbed. Nobody was on the path and, after catching her breath, Rachel got back onto her bike and continued on.

At an overpass, she dismounted and walked her bike across the bridge to the side of the river her encampment was on, and stopped. She no longer had the sense that she was being followed or even observed, but did not discount the possibility that these people had more sophisticated means of tracking and observing her. But, there was nothing she could do about that and hyper-vigilance had spent her energies. She locked her bike at *Bennie's*, a high-end hamburger restaurant, and went in. The total for a simple cheeseburger and fries was nearly triple that of a fast food drive in, but she was too tired to care about her budget. She chose a booth in the corner, by the window. A large, flat screen television was playing in the corner, but Rachel ignored it. She ate slowly, staying longer than would be prudent did she not desperately need the rest.

It was noon; her parents would be searching for her by now. She had to leave. Rachel went to the restroom and gave herself a quick sponge bath using handfuls of coarse brown paper towels from the holder on the wall. This was only the beginning of her day's exertions, she knew. The cold water revived her enough that she was prepared to leave.

From this point forward, she would operate on the assumption that she was being looked for. Rachel passed a sporting goods store. She needed some items to take into the woods, but there was too little traffic in such a store to be confident her visit would go unnoticed. Instead, she went to the *Walmart* down the street and stocked up on final items such as nutrition bars, toothpaste and toothbrush. It was for real now, and if she were going to survive in her mountain hideout, she'd better be prepared.

In the sporting goods section, a man and his son were standing in front of tents talking about a 2-man model, the same one she had purchased clandestinely a few months ago and cached in the woods. It was a small hiking tent with an extra, protective canopy over it.

"It's self-supporting," the boy said. "That could save time."

Before considering the wisdom of doing so, she stopped and said, "No, I have that tent. It is self-supporting, but I would still stake it down if there's any chance of a wind – and there's always a chance of wind. Up here at least."

"How do you like it, otherwise?" the man asked. He was shorter than his son but was well built, like a man accustomed to strenuous outdoor activity. He wore a brown and beige checkered shirt tucked neatly into his jeans and held in place by a brown leather belt with large, brass belt buckle with an eagle on it. She thought it looked like a belt buckle for an arms manufacturer, but the man didn't look like the type; not a hunter. She glanced at it again. It was for fishing of some sort, maybe a resort keepsake.

"It's great. It costs less than ones that aren't nearly as sturdy," Rachel answered.

"Where do you take it?"

She paused. She wasn't prepared for this question. It was foolish to have engaged someone in conversation. To do so about a tent, of all things, was lunacy. "Yellowstone."

"Have you been to the Lewis River?"

One lie leads to another. "No, we haven't gone yet, I've just set it up in my backyard a few times to try out. I've even slept in it once. Where are you folks going?" She added the last to steer the conversation away from herself.

"We're staying in the area, at first." The boy answered this time. He was about Rachel's age and, although taller than his father, had not filled out yet.

"Really." Rachel looked around.

"Yes, maybe do some gold panning. We're new to the area so the forest and river aren't old stuff to us. We do want to get up into the mountains a bit before there's snow."

"Good idea. It gets really cold in winter." Rachel wondered if she had truly considered just how challenging winter would be on her own in the mountains.

She didn't know what to say and tried to think of stock phrases to fall back on. Yet, she wanted to talk with them, but wasn't sure why. Something about them; their relationship, which she could sense was a strong one based upon mutual respect and consideration.

"Well, I have to go. Enjoy your trip," she said, standing there motionless.

"Well, Eric, we'd better get checked out," the man said. "Thanks for the tip."

"Yes, thanks," the boy answered, but made no move to leave.

"Thanks again." The man hefted the tent into their cart. The boy smiled at her as they walked away.

Rachel looked back at the man and his son before heading to the checkout. Were the circumstances any different, she would have stayed with them longer. The father's easy manner and the son's friendliness had brought her back to life for a moment, rekindled the social instinct which was dormant, but still alive, within her.

She needed to ditch her bike soon, but the store parking lot would be a very bad choice as its discovery could lead to an investigation of her purchases within and provide clues as to her intentions. After exiting the lot, she left the bike by the side of the road. Surely someone would come across it and take it for themselves and it would not be traced back to her. Such an abandonment was harder to do than she had thought it would be; she grew up with privation and having a bike, an American bike in America, was a greater boon to her than winning the lottery would be to most people. Rachel turned several times to look at it as she walked off, the red paint reflecting the sunlight that shone through the break in the clouds after the morning's rain subsided. It had probably been the last rain of the season. Most of spring and all of summer was ahead of her. Creatures following her or not, she doubted she would have risked camping in the Sierra Nevadas in winter. She would use the time to prepare and, perhaps, build a more permanent shelter before the weather turned cold and the first flakes of late fall or early winter snow fell. Her load was heavier as she was now carrying her purchases in addition to the garbage bag containing the food and water she had packed at the house.

***

"Can't get her out of your head, eh?" Eric's father asked him as they drove home from the sporting goods store.

"No."

"Well, there was something about her. Definitely."

"Do you think she's Russian?"

"Maybe, but more likely Gypsy or Romanian." He shrugged his shoulders and continued, "Or she could be a mix of both. I don't think she's Slavic."

As they turned onto the overpass that would take them to the freeway entrance, they saw her walking, backpack on her shoulder, and carrying her bags of purchases from the store.

"Should we offer her a ride?"

"If your mother were here we might, but not alone. You just can't take that risk these days. Plus we do have to get back." He said and looked at her from his rearview mirror. Her figure was becoming smaller and less distinct as the distance between them widened, and as she disappeared, he hoped they would encounter her again.

Eric watched her until they made the turn onto the freeway entrance that would take them home and she was no longer visible.

Chapter 9

Rachel wished she could take a bus back the direction she had come, for in fleeing from the Blue Dress People, she had overshot her destination. But she didn't know the routes here and being on a bus would trap her if they decided to take her now that she was fleeing, or if her parents had already gotten the word out to the police that she was missing. More than a few church members were in law enforcement and her parents could have a search initiated very quickly. She began walking. When able, she avoided areas where she could be spotted easily from a passing car. The rest of the day passed rapidly and it was growing dark as she entered the woods on the path that led in the direction of her camp.

The way was treacherous at night and after stumbling several times on the slick ground, she realized she would not be able to make it to her cache safely, which was still several miles away, and must stop and make camp for the night.

She chose the most secure area she could find: an alcove in the rocks by the river she remembered from earlier scouting expeditions. The only approaches were from the path up, which wasn't really even a path, it was so rough, and from the river, which formed its own barrier. The stone shielded her from view from the other two sides and she would be able to see someone coming before they got close. The stone floor where she set her packages was also recessed enough to cover her from the view of any passing river vessels. Exhaustion concerned her, and Rachel was worried that a sleepless night would leave her in a poor position for the next morning's hike. However, as she lay on a hastily made bed of garbage bags stuffed with leaves to protect her from the cold, wet ground, she found that her worry had subsided and she fell asleep almost upon closing her eyes.

Rachel awoke to the gray of early morning. From her position she could only see patches of the river through the morning mist. I must be careful walking was her first thought – it would be so easy to trip on some branch or rock and fall into the water. It was cold and she was still damp from her hike and a drizzle that must have occurred during the night. She brought the blanket closer and pulled herself into a fetal position. Her body was sore all over and, despite the hours of sleep, Rachel felt wasted. There could be no harm in just lying here for a moment; she dreaded getting up to the cold. From through the fog, she heard a bird whooping and a moment later a small splash – a fish jumping, a frog? Snakes could swim and Rachel feared them. What if one had been drawn to her warmth in the night? They had been known to slither into sleeping bags and biting campers when they stirred. Rachel shivered, wishing she could channel, but settled for feeling her body from feet to shoulders, sensing for any bumps or foreign objects. Nothing.

She had to get to her camp today and couldn't stay here much longer even if she didn't want to move from the bed her body had warmed and into the cold, foggy air. Through the branches, she could hear a duck making its way through the water. For an instant she saw it as it passed the point where the mist broke. The early day muted the brown and gold hues of its feathers but its silhouette was clear and if that were not enough to identify it, it began quacking, setting off the silence of the morning by contrast.

She forced herself to sit up and with the most economical movement possible, holding her arms tightly to her chest and shivering, stood. Rest would come when she made it to her cache and set up permanent camp. Last night, she had only been disoriented from being chased; this morning she would find her way. The way to warmth was activity, she knew, and grabbed one of the halters on her pack and slung it onto her shoulders. It had been a long time since Romania and it privations, and the taste in her mouth from her un-brushed teeth was unpleasant. Chewing on pine needles could improve bad breath, she remembered, but did not stop to grab any as she made her way up the hill, carrying her load of food and water.

Careful, she lectured herself: a broken leg or even sprained ankle means game over. Rachel walked for less than five minutes before spotting the railroad trestle. If she followed it, it would lead her towards her hideaway. Why had she not seen it last night? It seemed impossible to miss, intersecting the river near where she had slept, and blocking the view of the woods from the floodway it had been built to cross. Floodway. This river had a tendency to overflow or they would not have spent the time and expense making the trestle. How could she have forgotten – or rather, not noticed – something that could so imperil her survival? And why had she allowed herself to become so soft, so used to creature comforts that she was as much, or more, worried by their absence as concentrating on her environment and survival?

At least the floodway made a relatively smooth valley to follow before entering the woods again. Still, she was out in the open and that was not good. She started to run, then slowed to a brisk walk for running would attract more attention than a solitary figure ambling across.

The field ended abruptly at the tree line. The ground rose before it and she had to walk along the edge a time before finding a path up. It was oblique and framed by small river stones. Her shoes were still moist and she had to lower her profile to keep her balance and measure every step before she took it but finally she was over it. She was met by a row of ferns and looked carefully to be certain there was no poison ivy before advancing. Fortunately, there was a path ahead. Not well used, but better than traipsing through undergrowth.

She walked for nearly two hours, stopping twice to rest and only for a few minutes each time. The fog had lifted to a slight mist and the exercise warmed her although the exertion was causing her to sweat – the hiker's bane, as it could contribute to hypothermia. Rachel wished she could change into dry clothes.

Ahead was a small outcrop from which she could check her location and the distance to the hills behind her house. It didn't look very far at all, but distances could be deceiving. She was about to set off when she saw something move in the field directly behind her neighborhood. There was a man – no, a man and a woman. The woman was bent over, probably tying her shoelaces; the man was waiting for her. Rachel stopped cold as the woman straightened up and they began moving in her direction. After a few minutes observing the pair, she was relieved to see them open a gate and enter a backyard some blocks from the Stephenson's home.

It was well into early afternoon before she located her cache. Despite previous plans of camping at that spot, she decided it would be more prudent to go further up the hill and deeper into the wilderness. She had never seen anyone up here before, but now that it was for real, she felt more cautious. Also, it would be wise to camp further up in the mountains to be on higher ground in case of flooding.

Another forty-five minutes passed before she had moved her stuff to what she judged to be a more secure hiding place. Large boulders formed a V she could back her tent up against as a barrier to approach from the rear, and the surrounding foliage was deep enough that somebody would have to walk within feet of the tent to see her encampment. Although in a minor valley, the camp was on the other side of the mountain from the river and she did not have fears of flooding from a swollen river. Rachel took several garbage bags from one of the duffel bags she had cached and spread them on the ground where her tent would be. Two deep at least, would be wise, as she might be here for a while and did not want to get wet or have the ground suck the heat from under her. She spread a layer of ferns and other foliage between the layers of garbage bags to serve as insulation and cushion, while remaining alert for hikers or Possessors and other magical creatures, yet acknowledging that any creature that managed to track her here would probably see her before she saw them. She worked quickly, but methodically, and was surprised to see it was late afternoon when she was done.

Evening would be here soon. She had better eat dinner and disguise her camp as best she could in the unlikely, but possible, event some hiker decided to explore this nook of the woods. A campfire would be too risky, at least until she had a sense of the area, so she took two Power Bars from her knapsack and munched on them as the light faded.

That first night, Rachel discovered that darkness with hills between her and the city lights and backed into a valley like this, was quite dark indeed, and would have been frightening even without the fear of being stalked. The woods held many unfamiliar sounds. Sometimes towards nine o'clock, she heard some rustling around her camp. She started, but it was too light to be a human which would break the twigs and branches she had spread about to provide an alarm of approaching hikers or, should she be tracked by the police, searchers. Even so, she flipped off the camping light and stayed motionless, lying on her sleeping bag. It was too overcast for moonlight and, peering carefully through the opening in her tent, she could see little but the silhouettes of the trees, rocks and foliage. Rachel wished she could channel, to use the Power, to sense what was outside, but she did not dare. Any use of the Power could signal her location to the Blue Dress People.

This was going to be harder than she thought.

By midnight, Rachel regretted fleeing. But what could she have done? Stayed with her parents? Okay, she could have done that, but what about those things following her? Could they not get her here just as easily? And with no witnesses? But no, intuition suggested, that in fleeing, she had broken their tail. If she did not channel beyond a careful minimum, and that, only when far from camp, they might not ever find her. It had been her early careless experimentation that brought her to their attention. If only she had known six months ago what she now knew. But what about Katie? The tiny witch wouldn't know where she had gone – Rachel had never thought to tell her the exact location of her cache. Besides, she had moved from the original spot, anyway.

Yet, somehow, Rachel knew, the mountain witch would find her. Not on Rachel-time, but on Katie-time. When the little witch decided it was time to visit with her friend, she would, and Rachel didn't think location mattered so much with Katie. The two had a bond of some type. Still, she wished her friend was here.

She lay, dressed, on the sleeping bag for an interminable amount of time until, finally, sometime during the night she dozed. It was still dark when she woke, but she could see the early traces of the coming dawn: the trees were no longer simply silhouettes and she could pick out individual branches. She had made it through the first night. In a couple more hours, she could start the day and make her settlement more secure and comfortable.

Chapter 10

"Hey, Charlie, what is this?" Candice asked Detective Charlie Webb. She held up a Missing Person's case file. A pink post-it note was attached from Detective Lieutenant Bill Price, her and Charlie's boss, asking her to take a look at it. "Bill left in on my desk."

"He wants you to take the lead on the Stephenson case. Poke around some."

"What does your gut say, Charlie? Is this another 'ThinkingOfYou' case?"

"Doubt they're related, but stranger things have happened. I saw the girl's parents when they came in to report their daughter missing. They certainly thought she took off on her own initiative, but you never know."

"You checked out her school, didn't you?"

"Yeah. Girl had few friends. A bit of a wallflower. Nobody knew of anybody she was seeing and no one knew her well enough to have friended her on any social networking sites or even have her cell phone number."

"Well, with four girls missing already, this one goes under the microscope." She picked up the file and sat at her desk: an old oak model with half a century or more of mileage on it. Like most things in the building, and even the building itself, their office was a hodge-podge of scavenged furniture acquired piece-meal from government surplus. This didn't matter to Candice, just so long as her computer worked and was up to date. Much of her job now revolved around accessing databases – including the FBIs' Vi-CAP database, the system designed to track and correlate information on violent crime, including murder, sexual assault, and missing persons where foul play is suspected. The system utilized modern technology and was particularly valuable in tracking serial killers; killers who often crossed jurisdictions, leaving local police otherwise unaware that a case in their region could be connected to incidents in other regions.

This was what puzzled Candice. Serial murder was considered sexually and control driven and with a specific "signature" that evolved over time. Unlike M.O., or modus operandi, the method by which the predator commits the crime, i.e., gun, knife, etc., the "signature", or what the killer or sexual predator "gets" out of the crime, tends to stay constant, even if its manifestations evolved. Yet, they did not know what "ThinkingOfYou" did with the missing girls.

She opened the file. Clipped to one of the pages was the photograph taken in Romania by the adoption agency. Staring at Candice was a young girl of eleven or twelve. Her eyes were blue and her hair was coal black. She was wearing a gray dress that would not have been out of place in a mid-19th century orphanage or workhouse of the type Charles Dickens wrote – except for a pink ribbon tied into her hair. Where had she gotten that? Must have fashioned it out of a scrap of cloth she found somewhere. Still, despite the obvious poverty, the girl's eyes were defiant. Not like the proverbial deer caught in the headlights, Candice would have expected from one in such a cruel environment, but more like a cougar's – frightened, wary, ready to fight.

The Communists under Ceaucescu had encouraged fertility well beyond what the society could support. The result was a surplus of children, large numbers whose parents could not care for them. This "surplus" had been housed in orphanages under horrific conditions. Although this girl had been born after the fall of the regime, the system remained broken for years even after the revolution. Somehow this girl had dodged the starvation, unsanitary conditions, illnesses, such as HIV and tuberculosis, as well as the brutal beatings and sexual assaults so many children suffered in orphanages during that time in Romania. And then, apparently, she had escaped from one of these warehouses of child death and lived on the streets before being taken in by a privately run charity orphanage. Yet, despite all of this, the girl, Rachel, was actually one of the lucky ones. Or lucky ones up to this point. That this girl had survived such an early life spoke volumes to Candice.

Chances were this fifth girl had been a runaway. Her parents had restricted her computer use to school tasks. Consequently, she had little Internet activity and no contacts with any user called "ThinkingOfYou", nor with any other unknown persons.

None that they were aware of. Forensics had also checked the computers at Rachel's school as well as those at the Melville library – but that did not rule out other sources of Internet access.

Investigators had also gone through her cell phone, but found only a handful of text messages and all were from relatives, most instructing her to do this or that, or go here or there. Commands.

Yet this girl, or young woman, had some similarities to the other four missing ones. Rachel Stephenson had family problems and been socially isolated. She could have been vulnerable to a predator masquerading as a friend. A neighbor had seen her leave the Stephenson's home alone, and on a bike. She had also left her parent's car keys on the kitchen table. Did she leave to meet with someone?

Candice's gut reaction – and her fourteen years as an investigator had told her to listen to her intuition – told her there was a connection here. She made copies of the original report and Charlie's interview with the Stephensons and put it into her briefcase. Reports could only tell so much. It was time for her own interview with the parents.

The deciduous trees, that turned parts of Northern California into a festival of blossoms in spring, lined the road toward the Stephenson's house. Magnolias with their soft pink blossoms, reminding one of a Japanese garden, and dogwoods with their paper white flowers, punctuated by contrasting shades in their styles and filaments, were in full bloom. Residential neighborhoods such as these often preferred smaller trees such as dogwoods to the evergreen pines, pines with deep green needles and hearty trunks, but trees which could, when weakened, land on a roof during a storm. The winter rains had just ended, yet sprinklers, were already in action in many front yards. Candice turned the corner onto the street where the Stephensons lived. It was lined with mostly single story homes, which, nice as they were, gave way to larger, more ornate double story models further down the street. The neighborhood was still relatively new, but all but a few houses here and there were occupied, with bikes and children's toys out front.

Candice had deliberately chosen a Sunday to meet with them: the closer the conditions were to the day of Rachel

Stephenson's disappearance, the better, and Candice had known of more than one case that was solved by this very sort of attention to detail. Methodical was the way to go. Shortcuts ended up being the long way around in the end.

She saw the house and knew it was the one she was looking for, but instead of pulling into the driveway, passed it by. Better to get a feel for the neighborhood - it would help her to ask better questions.

At the corner, she turned. On the right side a small park, bisected with well-worn paths, ran from the curb all the way to the levee in back. The grass was bright green and recently mowed; tan painted wooden stumps at equal distances formed a barrier between the park and the sidewalk and a large jungle gym with slide, swing set, rings and a fort like log citadel, offset slightly from the center of the landscape, formed the largest structure. Further away, past the sand lot, were a number of tunnels for kids to play in, or, as Candice noted, for someone to hide in. A mother was pushing her young son on a swing.

A Lexus SUV parked at the curb. It probably belonged to the mother. So, this is a better neighborhood than she'd thought – a place where top of the line SUV's were standard – and children were ornaments. She stopped herself. Not fair to pre-judge these people. It wouldn't help the case. Old resentments from the rough economic times her family suffered after the factories in Detroit, where her father and uncles had worked, went fallow in the 1970's, were not relevant here. The accountants, middle managers, and other white collar professionals employed in the auto industry, had also been left scrambling to find employment just as her father, an engine builder, had. Mike Strong had worked for 27 years at the same auto factory, only to get a pink slip and a letter from Corporate that expressed regret that "the changing business environment" had rendered it necessary to move his and his coworkers' jobs overseas. Well, they hadn't really said that about moving the jobs, but it was common knowledge that was where the work was going.

She had meant only to drive by on an initial reconnaissance of the neighborhood, but, instead, found herself pulling up at the curb, half a dozen yards behind the Lexus and walking the block on which the Stephensons lived. On foot, one could see things that were not apparent from inside a car, and Candice immediately noted the side gate of their house was shielded by trees and the neighbor's raised landscaping. The girl had been seen, by a neighbor, exiting here on her bike. Why had she not chosen the other gate, the one next to the garage door? Or why not the garage door, itself? Didn't the girl keep her bike inside the garage like most kids? Was there an alarm door on the garage and did Rachel Stephenson take the gate to avoid tripping the alarm? If so, why did she not use the gate closer to the garage? Did she not want to be seen, and if not, by whom? Her parents were still at church at the time.

Candice continued walking until she had seen all she could without entering the house and speaking to the girl's parents. She had some new questions for them. Good interviews were usually good because the investigator had done his or her preliminary work. One powerful way to ascertain the candor or truthfulness of a witness was to ask them a question you already knew the answer to and see how they responded.

She knocked on the door. Footsteps sounded on the bare wood floor within. The chain was pulled back inside and the door opened to present Janice Stephenson. Mrs. Stephenson was well dressed in a businesslike dark brown skirt and cream blouse. Her blond hair was shoulder-length and neatly trimmed. Candice knew they were expecting an investigator and wondered if the Stephenson's had dressed for her. That could be telling.

"Detective Strong." Candice presented her credentials. She saw the husband through the doorway as he entered into the hall. He was dressed in a business suit with tie, but his jacket was not on.

"Please come in," Mrs. Stephenson said and for a moment, the three stood crowded in the hall by the door.

James Stephenson stepped back and motioned them into the living room. "Please have a seat. Make yourself comfortable."

Candice noted the rise in pitch in Mr. Stephenson's voice as his sentence ended. This denoted nervousness, but Candice was well trained and experienced enough to know that nervousness didn't necessarily signify deception. Too many pop psychology books had led to people believing such nonsense that if you raised the pitch in your voice, touched your hair, stroked your legs in a pacifying manner, or moved your body inward to lower your profile, that you were automatically lying or hiding something. No. The very same behaviors could also indicate fear or apprehension for other reasons than fear of discovery or discomfort in lying; such as being arrested for the first time, whether innocent or guilty, being caught in an embarrassing situation, or having a police detective visit your home for an interview.

The room was well furnished with real mahogany, maple, and cherry tables and cabinets. In the corner a display case held crystal pieces, Lladro figurines, fine dining glasses, and Faberge eggs. So, these people had good tastes – expensive tastes, but not necessarily above upper middle class level. A family portrait hung over the main sofa. Over the sofa, it could not be easily seen by those seated inside the room as it would be behind those seated there, and the other, smaller sofa, was at an angle facing away from it. So, was it there for effect? Wouldn't they want it where they could see it? This could mean something, or it could mean nothing. In any case, Candice noted it.

There was also a framed photo montage on the side wall. Rachel at a family trip to Disneyland at about age thirteen. Then the pictures of family scenes tapered off to simple studio portrait prints. So they had the requisite props, but Candice had seen enough in her law enforcement career to know that family pictures prominently displayed did not mean the family was close or not deeply dysfunctional. In fact, many of the worst parents she ever encountered in the course of her work were those who displayed pictures of their "happy family" for all to see: in their office, in their home and in their wallets.

Did something happen to change their relationship around that time, around the time the girl turned fourteen? Did the Stephensons become bored with being parents after the novelty wore off?

"What we have been through; I wouldn't wish that on anyone," the mother said after which her husband put his arm around her and pulled her closer.

Not what sort of peril our child could be in, what she could be going through, only what *we* are going through. Candice noted the implicit narcissism in their response. Their life was disrupted; they had to deal with worry and uncertainty. Candice asked them the necessary questions and got the expected answers. No, their daughter didn't fit in well at either school or church. No, it wasn't their fault and, no, they didn't think their daughter was in communication with anybody outside her church, school or family circles. Only twice in the more than hour she spent in their home did they mention concern over what their daughter could be going through. The only item of interest to Candice was their puzzlement as to why their daughter would have used the far side gate to exit.

Chapter 11

After a quick breakfast of a nutrition bar and nuts, flushed down with some of her precious water, Rachel risked a trip to the river to wash. She selected a pair of baggy, but sturdy, jeans and a checkered lumberjack style shirt – something she'd never wear at home – from among the bag of clothes she had purchased at thrift stores over the past several months for her cache. Rachel added a man's wool sweater over it all, then fastened her hair up with a piece of twine she used as a ribbon and covered it with a baseball cap pushed down as far as it would go. Another means of disguise. She did not leave camp until she was satisfied that someone seeing her from a distance would find her difficult to recognize.

She didn't enter the path above her little valley until she was certain no one was there, then, like a deer making a quick break through open, vulnerable ground, she crossed to the opposite side of the path where there were more trees and undergrowth for her to duck into should she need to take cover.

Her precautions turned out to be unnecessary as she saw no sign of other campers or hikers and she had a refreshing wash in the river.

Days passed. Rachel settled into a routine, rarely used her light at night anymore and read during daylight hours. Now, more of a woodsman, much of her fastidiousness had gone. True, she did brush her teeth regularly and wash her hair at least every other day and, on those days when it wasn't convenient to take a dip in the river, took at least a sponge bath; but no longer did the lack of home comforts bother her so much.

Within a few weeks, the novelty of living in the woods had worn off and she was making serious progress with her math and science books. Most were older editions of college texts she had purchased at thrift shops, but the basic laws of classical mechanics had not changed and calculus was the same as it had been since long before the oldest books she owned were written. When she exhausted her current stock – and Rachel reckoned she could get through four to six months of study eight hours a day before that happened – she would have to go into town for some more. Not her town, though. She would make an expedition and follow the river until it reached the next population center, find a bookstore, and dash in and out with a new supply of texts. That was still a long way off, and she set aside the problem for later consideration.

Her camp was in the valley between the foothills in the South and the mountains in the North. Clouds rolled in, set off by the brilliant ultramarine blue of the sky. Someday, when she had full control of her Gift, she would command them, paint shapes in the sky with them, cause them to shadow one area and illuminate another. The sunsets here, not obscured by the city, were more dramatic and she made sure not to miss these. As the weather turned warm, she did not have to bundle up so much to watch them as she had her first days.

It was at times like these Rachel wondered about her own history. How had she been Gifted with the Power? Katie had suggested she was born with it. Who then were her parents? Was the Gift passed down from one generation to the next? Did it skip generations? If her mother had had the Power, why had her daughter ended up an orphan – in conditions of extreme poverty and neglect?

She had forgotten her amethyst gemstone, but not her hairbrush. The stone might have been useful in her studies, but the brush meant more to her as it was the only connection she had to the one brief period of happiness in her life. For the moment, though, she did see how understanding the principles of reflection and refraction would help her. Concentrating a light into a single point of reflection to bounce it at a threat, could momentarily stun a creature, but the Possessor had been too agile and difficult to see that she did not believe she could use it effectively against one. The Blue Dress People could probably counter such a tactic easily.

One afternoon, while reading about resonance in the college physics book, Rachel decided it was something she would like to try. She felt secure enough now, after weeks without any appearance of her stalkers: either the Blue Dress People or Possessors. The idea behind resonance is that force applied to an object in just the right rhythm would make it vibrate. For example, pushing a child on a swing at the right rhythm will make her swing very high. The frequency at which you push the swing is its resonant frequency. The physics book mentioned the Tacoma Narrows Bridge, which collapsed in 1940 due to vibrations caused by a wind that was only a third as strong as those the bridge was supposedly designed to withstand. The wind had hit the bridge at precisely the right speed and angle to initiate the vibrations that grew to tear the bridge apart in only a few minutes. Every structure has its own resonant frequencies, which depend on the geometry and construction materials of the structure. Making a building earthquake resistant is about being attentive to its resonant frequencies.

If Rachel could direct her power at an object, perhaps a rock or tent peg, so that the force on the object oscillated at its resonant frequency, she could destroy the item in this way. It would open up new possibilities for her. She wouldn't have to harm another creature.

Instead, she could protect herself by causing objects to break and fall in a pursuer's path, blocking their way. Or perhaps she could damage a car, making it inoperable. There were many possible uses for such a skill.

The book stated:

> Earthquake resistance is about being
> attentive to an object's resonant frequency.
> A large object can be moved by a small
> force if the force is applied with the right
> rhythm based upon the object's geometry.

She did not think these magical people, whatever, or whoever, they were, intended to physically harm her, but they did intend to use her in some way and that way might not necessarily be in her interests or in keeping with her own moral sense. Rachel would feel safer with another arrow in her quiver of self-defense techniques.

She grabbed a pebble from the ground near her tent and allowed the faintest trace of the Power to channel from her towards it. She stopped. Not here. Not where I live. Best to go somewhere well away from her camp first. Rachel put the pebble in her sweater pocket and moved the foliage she had gathered over the previous weeks and used it to add more camouflage to her campsite.

Sometimes she wondered about the Stephensons. She had never written that letter saying she was leaving. Maybe it would've been better if she had. Well, it was too late now and anyone who really knew her situation wouldn't have a hard time believing her to be a runaway. Nevertheless, the absence of Katie did worry her. In the more than three weeks Rachel had been on the mountain, the witch had not paid a visit. There had been some scampering outside the tent at night, but Katie only let you hear her if she wanted you to, and Rachel could see no reason for the mountain witch to come to her camp without making herself known. If for some reason she had, she would have done so entirely unheard and unseen to Rachel.

She remembered the notes she had taken from Katie:

> Supernatural is a contradiction in terms.
> There can be nothing outside of nature
> and reality; it only appears that way
> because one's knowledge or means of
> perception is not adequate to see the
> multitudinous dimensions, combinations
> and permutations of physical principles
> that exist.

If Katie believed this, then Rachel's work with science should unlock the doors of the Power as it had done for the little mountain witch.

Rachel made her first, tentative, attempt at destroying a pebble with the Power on the banks of the river two miles upstream from her camp. The spot was blocked from view on three sides by trees and boulders that jutted out from the banks. The water was calm near the shore in the small bay the landscape had created. Hundreds of blue and gold minnows swam in the water and the soft, rhythmic sound made by the current lent a pleasing charm to the site. Despite being effectively hidden from view, she could see nearly indefinitely in both directions. Nevertheless, her caution caused her to channel such a small amount of the Power that she wasn't really sure if any was coming out at first.

After half an hour of such work, channeling small amounts towards the pebble, with the only noticeable effect being a slight, nearly imperceptible warming of it, she resolved to try a few times with a minutely larger amount of the Power. The bright, afternoon light had faded to a soft glow and Rachel knew she should be heading back soon or be caught walking through the woods at night. Also, she wanted to be gone quickly from the site after channeling, in case any witch was in the vicinity. This meant the final attempts could be the strongest. She would do it then hurry away.

Rachel laid the pebble near the water's edge and retreated behind the cover of the rocks and trees that lined that part of the bank. She inhaled a large breath then let it out as she directed a stream of energy at the pebble. It jumped. Too much.

The second time she tried with less and alternated the intensity up and down like the sine wave that described what her textbook called mechanical oscillation. The pebble started a few millimeters towards the water but did not move further. It bounced up and down and right to left in a dance reminiscent of a popular TV commercial for breakfast cereal. After what seemed like several minutes of concentrated effort, but what her watch told her was only about forty seconds, she dropped her focus and let the power dissipate.

"Ouch," she cried when she attempted to pick up the pebble. It was as hot as a smoldering piece of charcoal from the backyard grill and Rachel nearly fell into the shallow water when she jumped backward.

With the toe of her shoe, she pushed the pebble into the water a few inches to allow it to cool. After a minute, she put a finger in the water and gingerly touched the pebble. It was still a little warm, but no longer hot, so she took it out of the water and put it in her pocket. She would have to examine it later; the sunlight was fading and she knew she would have to move quickly to get back to camp safely before dark – and before any magical creature her channeling may have summoned came to the river to investigate.

It hadn't quite worked, but this heating up a substance in this manner could have definite uses. Imagine turning the ground, in a circle around her, too hot for someone, or something, to penetrate without being burned? Or using hot rocks to warm water as her primitive ancestors had? There was much to think about.

Despite the passage of time and the cessation of the terrors of the first night, she remained careful whenever leaving or entering camp, and was particularly so this time. The light had visibly dimmed when Rachel made it back and set her warning sticks out for the night.

The foliage used for insulation under the tent was no longer soft after weeks of her sleeping and moving over it, but by now she was used to hard ground, and while no longer a cushion, it still kept the cold earth from sucking the heat from under her. Before the light fully died, Rachel took out her physics book and refreshed herself on the text about resonance. She must try sound waves soon. Mechanical vibration by way of the Power was too limited and was line-of-sight only. How sound waves could be generated and used, she did not know, but there were creatures called "Screamers" in Katie's book. Screamers transmitted their power by sound waves; hence the name, "Screamers". Somehow, she would make it work, she was sure, as the afternoon's slight success added to her weeks remaining safe and undiscovered gave her confidence in the future.

That evening, during the final moments of sunset, she sat on the promontory by her tent and looked out across the valley. The hills and trees in the immediate distance were crimson tinged. Further off, they were purple-blue, and farther still, where the landscape met the horizon, they were a full, soft, ultramarine blue and the sharpness of the hills and trees was softened to such a degree that one could not fix the exact point where the edges met. This was beautiful. It had been right to leave. I will survive and now I am free. As the sun set, and stars became visible in the evening sky, it reminded her of Vincent Van Gogh's "Starry Night" painting.

As Rachel retired into her sleeping bag, she again thought of Katie. She should have appeared by now. Where was the little witch?

Chapter 12

Eric was setting the dinner table. "Dad thinks we should follow the Melville River and camp in the mountains around it," he told his mother.

"It would be good to be near the river so you don't have to keep making water runs. Just don't fall in," she laughed. "It will be hard to get lost if you have it in sight, though. You can always follow it back. Just remember your pills and boil it anyway!"

"We know all about giardia," he answered, speaking of the protozoan parasite often found in contaminated water.

"You do? Well that's good." She smiled and patted his shoulder then went to the stove to check her roast. "Of course you do. I just worry."

"Get the TV, would you, Eric?"

He went into the living room and searched for the remote. The news was on. The broadcaster was speaking:

"A Melville girl is still missing after three weeks. Police say that 16-year old Rachel Stephenson walked off during a church service a week and a half ago and has not been seen since. Investigators believe the girl was distraught and left of her own accord. However, they are considering her an endangered runaway."

On the left sight of the television anchor was a picture of Rachel. Her hair was braided at the back of her head and she wore an ankle length dress with flower-patterned apron in the front. Eric recognized the obsidian black hair, sea-blue eyes and delicate face.

"Mom, Dad! Come quick! I know this girl, we saw her in Walmart a few weeks ago!"

The TV anchor continued, "Right now, despite some similarities in the cases, police are not yet considering her to be a possible victim of "ThinkingOfYou", but authorities are not ruling anything out at this time. Her parents are asking the community to keep them in your prayers."

"That is her. What day did she disappear?" Dan Edwards asked, moving closer to the television.

"Sunday."

"Did they say what time?"

"No, they just said she disappeared from church after the service," Eric answered.

"We have to find out what time their service ends," Dan said.

"Why don't you just call the police? They'll have that kind of information and it really doesn't matter what time you saw her. If you saw her, the police will want to know," Mrs. Edwards broke in.

"We did see her," Eric said.

"I'm not doubting you did," his mother replied.

"After dinner, I'll call Richard down the street. He's a deputy sheriff and should be able to put us in touch with the right investigators," Dan said.

"Maybe you should go now." Mrs. Edwards was still holding the dish of steaming broccoli she had been carrying to the table when Eric interrupted her.

"You think it's time critical? After all, it has been almost three weeks and they don't think she was abducted, just a runaway," Dan answered.

"If she's mentally disturbed, she could have put herself in real danger. I think the sooner they find her the better. If she's still alive," Mrs. Edwards answered.

"You think she could be dead?" Eric turned to his mother.

"I didn't say I thought she was. It is always a possibility, though." She softened when she saw his look. "Probably not. Most runaways either return on their own or are picked up by the police at some point."

Eric lay awake late in his room that night. On the wall, over the bed, was the poster of Mount Kīlauea his parents had bought him during their hiking trip to Hawaii two years before. He still remembered that trip fondly as it was the one where he and his father had discovered their interest in hiking. His mother didn't want them to get too close to Kilauea as it was still an active volcano, but after reading about the 1790 eruption in the park literature they picked up at the Visitor's Center, Eric could not be dissuaded. After receiving assurances from both her son and husband that they would run at the first sign of trouble, she had assented – though she made clear she preferred that they hike on the inactive Kohala Mountain instead.

Eric recalled the story of the 1790 eruption whenever he heard "Kona Blend" being ordered at Starbucks. The eruption had occurred during a battle for succession. Chief Keōua Kuahuʻula, and his band were traveling around Kīlauea to Kaʻū, after battling the dominant chief, Kamehameha I. At least 80 Hawaiian warriors under Keōua perished and footprints preserved in the ash were supposedly of these warriors.

The warriors should have been getting the heck out of Dodge when the mountain started to erupt, and not trying to propitiate the God, Pele. Fearing they had somehow angered her, the goddess of fire and volcanoes, Keōua remained there for several days to bestow offerings in an attempt to appease her. As he often did, Eric muttered a thanks to his parents for raising him agnostic. His father, to copy a popular science fiction author, referred to him and his wife as "devout agnostics".

Eric had relished the risk the active volcano presented, or perceived risk, rather, as the odds of it erupting without preamble just when they arrived was minuscule. He picked up the piece of quartz he had taken off of the mountain as a souvenir. It amused him when his friends admired "his rock", as he knew that quartz, because it had a uniform chemical structure, was a mineral and not a rock.

He wondered what interesting souvenirs they would find on this next trip. Ever since they had moved to this Northern California city, where his father had taken a job as a biologist for the state and his mother as a teacher at the local elementary school, he had wanted to go into the hills. Deep. The ostensible reason may be fishing and gold panning, but aside from the food requirements satisfied by fishing – and his father preferred they take some of their food from the land as it taught self-reliance – neither activity truly excited him.

What did was the thought of standing on one of the mountains they could see from their home and looking out across the still relatively wild valley and more distant peaks. Mountain lions and bears still roamed these woods. His mother wouldn't let them have a gun in the house, but his father had purchased two canisters of bear spray and had a woodsman friend show him how to use them.

He knew his father probably now regretted not stopping for the girl at Walmart or at least finding more about her. His father was that way – he would have wanted to help if he had known she was in trouble. His quick jaunt to the neighbor's house, after his wife had pointed out the gravity of the situation, without even stopping to call first, and then his later silence at dinner told Eric this. Maybe it was memories of the little sister his father had once had. She had been four and a half when she died of meningitis. Memories of this little sister, his only sibling, waking up that night in bed, screaming from the pain, still haunted his father, he knew. His mother had once told him the story, but his father never went into it with him – or with anyone else Eric was aware of.

Chapter 13

The nutrition bars were nearly gone. Only two remained, and Rachel set these aside for an emergency. There was no way to avoid a trip into civilization for supplies, no matter how risky.

She lay in her sleeping bag, books beside her, and planned the trip for the next morning. The best way would be to travel during the day, make a camp outside of town, and, after disguising herself as best she could, run into a convenience store and buy as many provisions as possible. If she timed the visit to a period when the store was crowded, the clerk would not have the opportunity to chat or make inquiries. Just in case, she would fill her pockets with rocks that she could use as a diversion should discovery or capture be imminent.

While she had never destroyed so much as a single pebble by oscillation, Rachel had learned other, useful, skills. Skills such as throwing a rock in one direction with the Power, rebounding it on a surrounding object and having it fly in another direction of her choice. She could have half a dozen flying at once, and if she were under some sort of cover, it would be difficult, perhaps impossible, for any target to determine the source or direction of the bombardment. Should she run into trouble, magically thrown pebbles would create an excellent diversion and allow escape.

Several times during the night Rachel heard rustling in the woods not far from her camp, but now, familiar with the raccoons and other woodland creatures that made the forest their home, she did not stir. Once in the night, however, one of her warning twigs snapped. Either it was a larger creature, or the small animals were closer to her tent tonight than before. She peered out of the opening, but saw no movement in the darkness and after some time had passed with no further sound, fell off to sleep.

***

"Dad! Telephone." Eric peeked his head into the workshop where his father was poring over river charts.

"Hello." Dan Edwards answered the telephone in his office.

"Mr. Edwards?"

"Yes. This is he."

"Candice Strong. I'm a detective sergeant with the Melville Police. I'm following up on your report on the missing girl: Rachel Stephenson."

"Yes. My son and I believe we saw her at WalMart a few weeks ago."

"I would really like to speak with both of you, as soon as possible."

"My son is at work with me today on a school biology project. I'm a biologist. We could come by your station after work."

"I could come there. I'm on my way to lunch; perhaps we could meet, if you haven't eaten yet. Whatever works best for you."

"There's a coffee shop across the street." Dan replied.

"How does one o'clock sound?"

"One o'clock at the Melville Cafe. We'll be there. I've been out in the field today, so I'll be wearing khaki pants and a dark green shirt. I doubt there will be more than a few customers in there, though."

"Good. One o'clock, the Melville Cafe." Candice wrote down the time and place in her notebook.

"Was that the police?" Eric asked.

"Yes, a detective. We're going to meet her for lunch at one." Dan glanced at his watch. It was noon. "Let me wrap up a few things here and then we'll go."

***

Rachel stood at the tree line and watched the traffic go by on the interstate, glad the hike from her mountain camp had been much shorter than anticipated. Seeing people, just being around them, was a welcome change after weeks of isolation.

She tightened the twine securing her hair up and pushed her baseball cap down. Several hundred yards from her position stood a convenience store. Dozens of customers had gone in and out in the twenty minutes she had been watching it. There should be little fear of her being noticed.

Rachel took her knapsack off, hid it behind a tree, and started walking towards the traffic light ahead. She slowed before reaching it, timing her arrival to coincide with a green light. To the right, a police car sped by, sirens screaming , blue lights flashing. She knew body language cues were noticed by experienced law enforcement personnel and avoided even the simple, nervous shift of weight that could be enough to attract a second glance. It took less trouble to appear nonchalant than she expected.

Nobody even glanced at her when she entered the store. The clerk was busy ringing up customers and the shelves she needed were in the back. Rachel grabbed a handful of Power Bars, a loaf of bread, and half-a-dozen packages of almonds and brought them to the counter.

In front of her, a lady was counting change, arranging the coins into piles of quarters, dimes, nickels and pennies. The total on the register was $6.35. Rachel breathed deeply. She was caught out in the open while this woman paid with small change.

The cashier waited, struggling to conceal his impatience, as the woman fumbled through her purse. He was an older man and Rachel wondered if this was a retirement job. She pretended to scan the shelves, looking for items of interest and avoiding eye contact.

"I don't got it," the woman finally said. "Can you take something off?" She stared at the cashier, then flicked the cellophane on a danish package. "This. I don't want this."

"Okay." The cashier voided the sale and rang up the rest of the items. "$4.23."

Two more customers entered the store. One glanced at Rachel as he passed. He was dressed in a preppy tennis outfit, a pair of sunglasses hanging in front. His hair was closely cropped and his posture erect. She hoped he wasn't an off-duty cop.

The cashier handed the lady her receipt and the customer grabbed her items without waiting for him to bag them and left the store without a word.

"You must like this stuff," the cashier remarked when Rachel set her Power Bars on the counter with the rest of her purchases.

"Not really. My brother does," Rachel answered.

"Can't stand them myself," the cashier said.

The man in the tennis suit was now behind her in line. From the mirror above the counter, Rachel could see him observing her. Fervently, she prayed he was just checking her out, guy to girl, and nothing else.

"$16.69." The clerk looked at her.

She handed him a twenty. He gave her the change and she hurried out. Next door, a blue sign said "Melville Café".

Rachel's courage was up. Why not a hot meal? Power Bars and lukewarm tea were getting old. And this coffee shop was secluded. Through its large windows she had a view of the parking lot in all but the back area – and that was for deliveries and employee parking. She could sit by the emergency exit and leave at any sign of trouble.

The lunch crowd was dwindling so Rachel had her choice of booths. She selected one in the far corner of the restaurant. From there, she could monitor the street as well as anyone entering. Overhead, fans leisurely spun. A song from the Carpenters played from the speakers and the scent of fries cooking confirmed to Rachel that the risk was worth it. Hot food!

She slumped in her seat, baseball cap off, but hair still up, and examined the menu. Something quick would be best. Hot, but quick.

"Hi, I'm Doug. Ready to order, or do you need some more time?"

"No, I'm ready." Rachel looked down at the menu. "I'd like a double cheeseburger with fries."

"Anything to drink?"

"Coffee, please. Oh, do you have soup?"

"Today's soups are clam chowder and chicken noodle."

"Chicken noodle," Rachel said.

"Chicken noodle it is. One cheeseburger, fries, soup and coffee. I'll be right back with the coffee."

Rachel wished she had brought a book with her. Maybe it wouldn't be wise to read when she needed to be on her guard, but she felt secure here. Even so, she fingered the pebbles in her pocket.

The food came, and Rachel had to exercise extreme self-discipline not to put the soup bowl to her mouth and drink it. Salt. That was what she had missed in her diet. If there was time, she would run back to the store and purchase some for her camp.

The fries were large, wedge size, and Rachel nearly burned herself when she shoved the first one in her mouth. Not willing to spit it out, she opened her mouth wide and breathed in, allowing the air to cool the half-eaten fry.

Outside, an olive Ford Taurus pulled into the lot. Rachel watched through her peripheral vision as a professional looking woman in tan slacks and blue blazer came out. When the woman glanced around, Rachel slouched further into her seat.

The lady checked in at the counter, but was not seated. Must be waiting for someone, probably for a business lunch. There was something about this that Rachel found vaguely alarming. This customer was erect, observant, and assertive. Not someone it would be good to be noticed by.

Another car pulled into the lot – this time a Toyota Prius. Inside were a man and a teenager. Rachel paid them no mind and continued watching the women as she waited. The windows encompassed the café and

Rachel had no difficulty seeing the front counter through reflections in the glass.

When the passengers of the Prius entered, the lady rose and welcomed them. She reached into her purse, pulled something out and showed it to them. The man glanced at it and moved to shake her hand. As the woman put the item back in her purse, it flashed gold. A badge.

Rachel forced herself not to bolt towards the exit. Nobody had noticed her yet; running would attract attention.

A waitress seated the trio in a booth by the wall near the front of the café. Rachel would have to pass directly in front of them to exit. Should she flee? No, she couldn't pass in front of the cop; police officers were trained to remain aware of their surroundings and the woman would surely look up. There was something vaguely familiar about the man and the boy, but their backs were to Rachel and she could not see their faces.

The woman excused herself and went to the restroom. Now was the time. Rachel took one of her last twenties from her pocket, grabbed the ticket and hurried for the front counter. The man and boy were talking when Rachel walked by their booth. She recognized the pair at once – the father and son she had spoken to at WalMart nearly a month before.

She turned so that her face would be away from them. However, they were immersed in their conversation and didn't even look up. Rachel waved the ticket and twenty to the waitress up front and laid it by the register. There would be no time to wait for change.

Out of the corner of her eye, Rachel saw the ladies restroom open and the woman exited. The police officer was now between Rachel and the front exit. Should she make a run for the emergency exit in back? These three could be meeting here about her disappearance, and they would surely recognize her. Was there some force at work here that brought the four of them together? No, she was being paranoid. Yet, what were the odds she would choose this very café at the same time they did?

Only seconds remained before the woman reached her. Dare she channel? Without making a conscious decision to do so, Rachel ducked behind the counter, channeled and sent several of her pebbles to the restaurant's far window.

Crash.

A shadow passed as the policewoman ran to the end of the dining hall. Rachel dashed out the front doors. Once out, she didn't run. The police would be looking for a rock-throwing vandal. What better way to cast suspicion upon herself than running? Plus, the rocks had impacted on the opposite side of the building and the policewoman would be looking there first. By the time backup arrived, Rachel would be back in the woods.

Still, she did not enter the forest at the same spot she had arrived. Instead, she passed the woods half-a-mile ahead and circled back under cover of the trees. Her pack was still there.

***

"No, this came from the inside. See here?" Candice pointed to the edges of the hole with her pen. "This is the entry point."

Dan and Eric looked at the holes. A uniformed patrol officer stood beside Candice.

"What could have caused this?"

"Was anybody back here?" Candice asked the manager.

"No. Nobody at all. My cook saw the impact, but he has no idea where the shots came from."

"What about the emergency exit?"

"It's alarmed and would have sounded if anyone opened it."

"Show me where the cook stood," Candice said.

She walked around the kitchen and stopped. Behind her, a delivery door was open to the right. Candice drew an imaginary line from the doorway to the broken windows.

"These could have been fired from this doorway. Would have to be three people with slingshots, though. A coordinated act of vandalism."

"Who would go through all that trouble to attack my restaurant?" the manager asked.

"Do you have any disgruntled former employees? Any customers you've had to ask to leave?"

"No. Not in years. There were some college kids my fry cook had words with when they caused a disruption: dancing on tables, screaming, and what not. But that was two years ago."

"Could be them, or it could just be some neighborhood kids playing a nasty joke. If you see anything strange, kids loitering in the back lot, etc., call us, okay?" Candice said.

"I will. This is strange. I've managed this place for fourteen years and I've never had anything like this happen before." The restaurant owner shook his head.

The patrolman took their statements and the manager signed a complaint. Candice returned to her interview.

"Now that was just crazy," Eric said.

"So she spoke to you about a tent?" Candice asked when things settled down and they were able to continue their interview.

"Yes. She said she had one."

"Do you remember any of her purchases?"

"I think she may have had a handful of Power Bars," Eric said.

"Also, I think she may have left a pack at the front desk while she shopped. I thought I saw her pick one up as we were leaving the store."

"Thank you, both. This has been some good information."

"Do you think she's okay?" Eric asked.

"Honestly? I don't know. I fervently hope so, but it is impossible to tell. We believe she probably left of her own accord. If that is the case, it is probably only a matter of time before she's picked up somewhere," Candice said.

They concluded their interview and parted. Candice handed both of them her card with instructions to call anytime if they remembered anything.

***

"Don't forget your extra socks!" Eric's mother called from the living room the day Dan and Eric left for their hike.

"I won't," Eric said from the hall. "Got 'em."

"We should have a good hike" Dan said to his wife after they had packed their gear into the car. "Say goodbye to your mother, Eric."

"Goodbye, Mom." Eric hugged his mother.

"Bye." She kissed him on the cheek. "Be careful."

"We will."

"Bye, hon." Dan said and kissed his wife. "See you soon."

"Bring some gold back!"

"We will," Eric said.

"Well, here we go," Dan said as he buckled his seatbelt. "Ready?"

"As ready as I will ever be," Eric answered.

Eric was too occupied with his own thoughts to notice the scenery as they passed the Melville River as it circled the edge of the town, the greenery in all its brilliance, nourished by the year's late rains, the historical buildings from the Gold Rush era, or the mountains rising in the distance, clear in the morning air. He felt in his coat to make sure the survival kit he had prepared, with his father's help, was still there. In it, he had a multi-tool, survival blanket, fish hooks and 100 meters of fishing line, whistle, and a signaling mirror. Folded inside his coat pocket was a copy of a map of the area they were going to hike. His father had laminated it and insisted they both become familiar with it and select meeting points for if they got separated.

As he ran through his equipment check, his thoughts turned to the girl, Rachel Stephenson. He could not forget her. What had happened to her? Had she met with foul play, or was she in a city somewhere with other runaways? He may have lived a sheltered life himself, but he knew enough about the world to know that bad things could happen to kids living on the street.

They parked their car in the secure lot at Dan Edward's workplace, a National Oceanic and Atmospheric Administration, or NOAA, fishery, where a coworker was going to return it to the Edward's house. Mrs. Edwards would pick them up two weeks later at the front gate. It was only about a mile from where they were going to enter the woods. They grabbed their gear from the trunk, secured the car, adjusted their packs and walked towards the bike trail that they would follow until it terminated at the foothills. Eric couldn't help but think they made a funny sight as they marched in full gear, packs and all, along the sidewalk at the edge of the town.

The bike trail would take them their first 8 miles, but after that, their journey would be on dirt trails up the mountain. Dan had planned it so that they would have a revitalizing lunch before they really started climbing in elevation. They had at least seven miles beyond the eight on the bike trail before they could make an encampment, but they were fresh and highly motivated and Eric felt they could make it with little problem. Father and son smiled at each other as they headed towards the hills. Both were pumped by their brisk walk and enthusiastic about their coming hike.

***

"Hello?" Candice answered her cell, after pulling over to the shoulder of the highway.

"Candice, it's Bill."

"What's up?"

"Need you to stop what you're doing and come in. There's been a development in the missing girl's case."

"I'm on the freeway. I can get there in about ten."

"Okay. See you then."

Candice pulled into the restricted parking area and made her way straight to Bill's office. What could it be? Had they found a body? She knew he would avoid saying something like that on a cell: they were careful about that – at least ever since the hacking incident in DC some years before.

When she entered his office, Bill was turned around on his swivel chair, rifling through some papers on the shelf behind his desk. There was a mirror behind him, so he saw her reflection before she announced herself. He stopped what he was doing and turned to face her. "Candice," he said without preamble, "we now believe that Rachel Stephenson had contact with the Unsub."

"I know," Candice said.

"You've heard?"

"No. I just felt it in my gut. Almost from the beginning. Heard what?"

"Her parents found a cell phone in their garage, stashed in a box of linen. They believe Rachel hid it there. She must have bought it with her own money when her parents took away her cell and computer privileges."

"Did it have anything on it?"

"Yup. A text message from 'ThinkingOfYou'," Bill answered.

There wasn't much to talk about, due to the dearth of evidence available in Rachel's case, but both agreed that

Candice should make another trip to the family home. But first she wanted to speak to Kimberly's friends and neighbors again, now that the cases were decisively connected.

Candice could see Mrs. Adams in the kitchen from through the window on the porch. The woman answered the door on the second ring.

"No news about your daughter," Candice said quickly, when she saw Mrs. Adams. The woman's mouth was open and her hand was at her apron sleeve, bracing herself for bad news. "I just need to ask you a few more questions, and perhaps take another look around."

"Are there any developments? Any news about my daughter?" Kimberly's mother asked.

"Not at this time. We do believe the person who contacted your daughter may have been in touch with another girl in the neighborhood."

"Please, come in." Mrs. Adams opened the door to admit the detective.

Candice stood in the hallway and filled her in on the basics of the Stephenson case, then asked if she could see Kimberly's room. Mrs. Adams led the way upstairs. "I haven't moved anything since that night. Just dusted and put everything right back as she left it."

"Thank you." Candice walked the perimeter of the room.

"So you're saying this other girl may have been a runaway?" Mrs. Adams asked.

"We don't know." Candice dug into her breast pocket. "Here is a picture of her. Do you recognize her? Could your daughter have known her?"

Mrs. Adams examined the photograph. "No. I haven't seen her before. Except on the news."

"Thank you," Candice said.

A thesaurus lay open on Kimberly's desk. Candice picked it up and flipped through it. Although there was nothing unique or unexpected about finding a thesaurus on a high school girl's desk, something about it caught her attention. She turned to the title page. A jolt of electricity brought her alert. She blinked once, twice. What the heck? For an instant, she thought she had seen an illustration of a minotaur on the page. Nothing there now but text. She blinked once more and took in the copyright date—1949.

Candice set the book back to its place on the center of the desk. On the shelf over the computer, was a modern set of reference books that included a dictionary, a grammar manual, and a thesaurus. Why did the girl have two?

Chapter 14

Pain awakened Rachel. It felt as if her neck and the back of her head were being crushed. She tried to sit up, but instead cried in agony and fell back onto her sleeping bag. She rocked herself slowly under the covers and brought her knees up to her chest in a fetal position. She tried to cry for help, even though a distant voice in her consciousness told her that help was too far away to hear. No matter, she could not manage more than a short gasp. The very act of moving brought what she already thought of as intolerable pain to an even more excruciating intensity. This was more pain than she had ever had in her life. Not even being beaten to unconsciousness, as a child at the orphanage, came close to this.

Please, God, let me die...

Every second was an eternity. The agony did not let up but she was exhausted by its attacks and could take in only shallow breaths. She tried to sleep, hoping to lose the pain in unconsciousness, but the illness pulled her back awake every time she felt herself going. At this moment, Rachel wished she had studied the life sciences

– and medicine specifically – as assiduously as she had physics.

Time. She couldn't judge time nor did she care about its passage. The afternoon sun beat relentlessly, warming the inside of the tent to near-inferno temps, but she did not have the strength to open the flap or even move closer to it. The air became stale and humid as the day progressed. Rachel put her hand over her eyes to shield them from the light. Sometime towards morning she had started to go in and out of consciousness but was only vaguely aware of this. Her mind was far in the distance, unreachable, while her body was a barely self-conscious zombie wracked by torture.

In the evening, she awoke lucid. The pain was still there, perhaps even greater than when it had first come, but the worst seemed to have passed – for the moment, at least. The valley was lit in the final stages of twilight. She knew that she could die if this continued. Though every movement was agony, she forced herself to pull the flap of the tent open and sucked in great gasps of fresh air. A modicum of strength returned. She must be dehydrated. All that sweating she did. Rachel inched her hand into her pack and groped for the canteen. It took nearly a quarter of an hour, but after dropping it several times and spilling more than she drank, she was able to get some water down. The water was warm – almost hot, and tasted awful. Forcing herself to drink was one of the hardest things she had ever done in her life. She did not have the energy to return the canteen to its place or even to screw the cap back on and simply let it drop onto the tent floor beside her head. The sun popped from behind a cloud. The added brilliance shot new bolts of pain through her eyes and into her brain. Before her head exploded, she closed the tent flap.

For the next two days, as she went in and out of consciousness, irrational nightmares and waves of terror overcame her. Several time Rachel felt that someone was in the tent with her and if she did not stay motionless, they would see her and harm her.

At twilight, Rachel awoke to find a rattlesnake curled beside her sleeping bag. Unable to move, she controlled her breathing and remained motionless. The warmth of her bed must have attracted it. She reached behind her head for her pillow. If she could get it before the viper struck, she could use it as a shield and roll out of the tent. She inched her fingers towards it, avoiding any sudden movement. The sleeping bag moved with her body as she turned, holding the pillow in front of her, and the rattlesnake dissolved into a zipper.

On the third night after the onset of her fever, the nightmares ended and she was lucid enough to sit up. Somehow she must have drunk from her canteen as it was now empty and the cap was screwed on. Beside it lay her knife, opened, blade locked. Had she drawn it in her delirium? Perhaps to fight against an imaginary, fever-induced foe?

Her bedding was wet; she must have relieved herself in the night. Rachel rolled the few feet across her tent and grabbed one of the plastic jugs she kept filled with water and drank a few sips. Afterward, she lay in her sleeping bag and stared at the ceiling of her tent. She no longer believed she would survive this illness.

Chapter 15

Eric and his father sat upon an outcrop looking out across the valley and across to the distant mountains. A pot of oatmeal was heating over their portable stove. His father had insisted they not cook where they slept, for fear of attracting hungry bears or other dangerous wildlife at night. Stone ground was also a safer place to start a fire. For, while they were very careful lighting the Sterno, the land around their camp was filled with dead leaves, branches, pinecones and other organic refuse, and there was always the chance of a spark starting a forest fire.

"This is beautiful." Dan rubbed his mittened hands together, steam rising from his breath.

"It's too early in the morning for beauty." Eric laughed.

"I think after it warms up a bit we can try a stretch of river and do some panning," Dan said. "If we start out after breakfast, it should be warming up by the time we find a place."

"Maybe we'll get a fish for lunch," Eric said. "That will save our food supply."

After eating, they took down the tent and packed their gear. The hike to the river took much of the morning as they stopped to take nature pictures of the mountains and any wildlife they encountered. Overhead, a hawk circled the mountain. Eric startled a rabbit as he turned the path near the river and it went hopping away, its brown fur camouflaged in the dried brush as it disappeared into the woods.

Gold is heavier than the dirt and sand that lines the river and creek beds, and as the water flows, the heavier gold dust and nuggets are deposited in areas where the current slows, such as around bends or behind obstructions like rocks, dead tree timbers and weeds. Eric helped his father select a portion of the river where the bedrock formed a cove and rich black soil lay underneath shallow water near the bank.

Eric stepped into the water, wary of the cold he was sure to come. In his hand he carried a pan for gold sifting. While it had the same general shape of gold pans of yore, of the California Gold Rush, the Klondike Gold Rush, the various Australian Rushes, his was made of modern plastics and colored light blue-green to better contrast the black magnetite sand that contained the gold dust and, hopefully, nuggets, from the riverbed.

Eric thought of himself as being in good shape. He was an experienced, frequent hiker, who practiced Taekwondo and wrestling and lifted weights in the garage with his high school friends to keep in shape, but the crouching, bending and scooping fatigued him in less than an hour and he found himself frequently standing to stretch himself and loosen cramps. From time to time, he could see the sparkle of gold dust, but it always disappeared as he swirled the pan to separate it from the dirt and gravel. It had seemed so easy when he and his father watched instructional videos on the subject.

"I would have thought these hills would have been stripped of all their gold years ago," Eric said. "Find anything?"

"Some dust, less than a gram, I think. Rains and erosion stirs up more, and the course of the river changes over time so there's always more supply. A century ago it extended further to the left." He nodded towards a sandbar across the river.

"Your luck is running hot, at least compared to mine, so you keep panning and I'll fish." Eric grabbed his pole to wade out into the stream.

"Be careful for snakes. Remember rattlesnakes can swim," his father answered.

Over the fire, they cooked two salmon that Dan had wrapped in tin foil and seasoned with wild dill found near the bank of the river. The scent of the fish was so inviting, that Eric put the first piece into his mouth before it had cooled sufficiently and he had to spit it back onto his plate. Steam rose from the meal as he moved the pieces about with his fork to let them cool.

Inside the tackle box, his father had fastened two pictures to the inside of the lid. One was their family holding fishing poles on a pier in Florida where they had just returned from deep sea fishing. At their feet lay a marlin, the evening light reflecting off its blue and silver scales. The second picture was much older; it was of Dan as a young boy of ten with his parents at the beach. Dan was beaming as he stood next to a sand castle he had just finished building. Kneeling beside him, with a plastic pail and shovel was a blond haired, blue eyed, little girl of three or four in a one-piece yellow bathing suit with ruffles of a type long out of style. This was his sister.

"No, it's all right. I was eleven years old when we lost her," Dan said when he saw Eric looking at her.

"I'm sorry. It's strange to think I had an aunt I've never met."

"She was a sweet little girl. Always exploring, asking questions. I had this electronic kit, and she would sit with me for hours as I worked on it, building radios, alarms, sirens, etc. I still miss her."

After lunch they continued to pan. Eric threw himself into it with increased effort, but at the end of the day, he had only a few flakes of dust while his father had filled a third of one of the vials they had brought to store their treasure. At least, that paid for the gear, he thought as they packed up for the day.

As they made the return hike to camp, Eric thought of his father and the sister lost so many years before and remembered the girl from the sporting goods store. Her image often came to him, not just her figure, which, as a teen boy in the midst of puberty attracted him, but also her voice, its enchanting Easter European accent, and a manner that blended both confidence and vulnerability. What had happened to her?

Chapter 16

The Sandman's coming in his train of cars

With moonbeam windows and with wheels of stars

So hush you little ones and have no fear

The man-in-the-moon he is the engineer

The railroad track tis a moonbeam bright

That leads right up into the starry night

So put on you 'jamas and say your prayers

The Sandman, Nursery Rhyme

Rachel was hearing noises outside her tent again. This time they were closer, within a few feet of the entrance, but she lacked the strength to investigate.

"Come with me," came Katie's voice. Just a whisper, as though it might be a continuation of the dreams she'd suffered the past few days.

"Katie! Where are you?" Rachel called. She knew Katie would find her!

"I am right outside," Katie replied.

"Where?" Rachel rolled forward, unzipped the flap and peered out. The air was clean, filled with the scent of pine and earth, and the valley was illuminated by the full moon. She could not see the little witch.

"Just stand up and come outside," Katie said.

"I don't think I can," Rachel replied.

"Yes. You can."

"I'm — I've been sick."

Rachel hesitated, then rose without the expected struggle to get her body to obey the commands of her mind; the soreness and exhaustion was gone from her. She stepped outside the tent. Katie stood above her, on the moss-covered boulder that formed the camp's enclosure. The moss was luminescent in a multitude of tones of green, blue-green and yellow-green, punctuated by slashes of yellow and gold ochre and shadowed in a cold, gray umber. Rachel stood mesmerized by the colors, and the clear night with its stars, and the trees and mountains silhouetted in the distance by the cool color of moonlight.

"Here, climb up." Katie patted the rock with her right hand. She was wearing her yellow little girl's dress and pink hair band in her golden hair.

"Wait, I have to go around."

"No. Use the stones as steps."

Rachel looked at the foot of the boulder where the mountain witch gestured. Several large stones on the side formed a nearly perfect staircase. How had she not noticed them before? They would have saved her an incredible amount of time whenever she left the encampment.

She took the first step warily, knowing it would be damp and probably slippery in the humid night air. It was not; her footing was firm, her body light and stable. Even so, she lowered her center of gravity and took the other steps carefully, if more quickly than the first. When she made it to the top stone, and climbed onto the boulder, Katie stepped forward and grabbed her hand.

Rachel felt a metallic snap, as of a padlock shutting as Katie took charge of her being. After weeks of isolation and days of hovering between life and death from illness, Katie was a lifeline. How could she have ever doubted her tiny witch friend would come?

For the first time in a long while, she felt free as the witch walked her towards the edge of the boulder overlooking the camp. Katie continued walking – over the edge. Despite the long fall ahead, Rachel didn't fight the bond and allowed Katie to lead her off the precipice.

Yet, they didn't fall, but kept walking, through the air, on some unseen support. Not flying, it wasn't that, they were just, well, walking. Rachel was no longer ill, and her body was in better shape that it had ever been.

In a handful of steps they were across the valley and climbing as if on some invisible ramp towards the stars. Katie said nothing, and Rachel was too busy watching the stars and the Earth go by as they ascended. In minutes, they were in the black of space. Not dark, though, as stars were on all sides. In front, suspended in the distance, was a jellyfish mosaic of gold, greens, blues, earth colors and a luminescent center which gave the colored cloud its brilliance.

A nebula? Like the spectacular pictures taken by the Hubble Telescope? Only this isn't a photograph, this was real and it was beautiful. Katie kept guiding her and Rachel understood they were making a loop around the nebula. Just as their turn put the formation to the right side, the witch stopped. Rachel wanted to ask what they were doing, but she did not. Katie stepped down, as if to tie her shoe, and took a portion of space in her hand and lifted it like a curtain. Beyond, there was more space. More, but this time the nebula was to the left!

It was also to their right. Two of them! How could this be? And what were they breathing? She could feel neither her breath nor the up and down movement of her chest, yet the hand she held was real. Life without respiration? Not quite substantial. A force field for witches? Was this within Katie's power? It must be, and Rachel realized this little creature was immensely more powerful than she had ever imagined. Why would she want an untrained girl such as Rachel for a companion?

"Let's go." Katie led Rachel through the curtain hole in space then returned the curtain to its place. Ahead was the mirror image of the sky they had just passed through. Had they entered into another world? The book Katie had given her spoke of parallel worlds. "You must never try this without me."

"Why? I wouldn't know how, anyway."

"You could tear the fabric of space and time traveling through worlds if you don't know what you are doing."

"So this is how you travel through worlds?"

"No, not quite like this. But this is best for now."

Katie led her along, for what seemed to Rachel to be an interminable time, through the dark lit by stars and other celestial objects. Finally, she stopped and told Rachel to wait. Wait they did for many minutes, holding hands and silently watching the sky. Then out of the blackness came a flash, as if from a nuclear detonation. Lights and colors filled all the area around them even though the epicenter was as far from them as the most distant visible stars.

"This is a supernova, isn't it?" Rachel asked.

"That's what you call it," Katie answered. "I wanted you to see it, so I took you back in time to the moment it occurred. I often come here myself, alone, to watch. I am glad to have somebody to share it with."

"Thank you." Rachel stood transfixed by the multitude of colors and values of light, "Thank you very much."

"We must go back, now," Katie said after some time had passed.

"Yes, in a moment."

"You can go back in time, Katie?"

"In a manner of speaking. I can observe but not participate or modify past events," Katie answered.

"My goodness. There is so much in the world I have been unaware of. Earth is so small."

"You come from a world where the great questions of conduct, knowledge and governance have all been solved by the dogma of religious bigotry, a bigotry that has closed off the great debate of life and the cosmos. You must let go these barriers and follow me into a world without limits, without boundaries."

"You sound like you're giving a college lecture." Rachel said, without removing her eyes from the scene before her.

"I am. I am speaking from the college available to all willing to leave the sight of familiar shore and journey into the unknown. Individual study and discovery. It is the only true school for those who wish to reach their full potential. Discovery with courage, and without limits and without pre-conceived notions of what one should find."

Was this what Katie had been trying to teach her all along? Why she hadn't spoon-fed her the answers? Because she wanted Rachel to ask these questions and search out the answers on her own, with minimal guidance, until she had learned to truly discover and progress on her own?

The return trip was much shorter, but Rachel was still too mesmerized by her experience to wonder about this. Back at the tent, Katie released the bond and Rachel found herself undressed, in her sleeping bag, with Katie nowhere to be seen. How had that come about? What had happened – a dream or real experience?

Rachel pulled back the tent flap and looked outside. Blue streaked across the sky, almost as from a flare, except that it remained as a line of flame, suspended in the sky. She wondered what this was, then fell back to sleep.

In her next moment of awareness, she opened her eyes. Two tiny, female figures stood in her tent. Another nightmare? But no, they were looking down at her and she felt no malice from them.

"We have come to bring thee to our village and restore thee to health," the taller of the two said. Mountain witches! So Katie had brought help, after all. Rachel smiled and drifted back into unconsciousness.

Chapter 17

C harlie had given Candice a list of witnesses who frequented the area where Kimberly, the missing girl they had the most case information on, was last seen. Most were transients, but one, a River Park maintenance chief was not.

Candice parked in front of the park office and maintenance compound. The area was small, hardly much bigger than two driveways side by side, and was surrounded by a tall chain link fence topped with razor wire. The razor wire wasn't really sharp as a razor, but did have barbs, and unlike regular barbed wire, razor wire, or tape, was difficult to circumvent without special tools and time. It was a significant psychological barrier, but she knew the area would have to be well secured after hours against vandalism and theft.

"Mr. Card, may I speak with you for a moment?" Candice displayed her police credentials for the maintenance chief. She held it still for examination and only put it away after he had a good look at it. In her experience, this helped build trust, sort of a polite request rather than an authoritarian press. She could do authoritarian, but had found that it was best held in reserve.

"Sure." Edgar Card leaned his rake against the utility shed in the maintenance compound.

"I am investigating the disappearance of Kimberly Daniels, a teen girl who went missing a year ago. We have reason to believe she may have met someone here the night of her disappearance."

"I know. I've spoken to the police many times. Even went to the station twice."

"Yes, I read the report. Thank you for your cooperation."

"What do you want to know?"

"You mentioned a homeless man who may have been in the park that night."

"Yeah, Stu. Haven't seen him for a year. I hope nothing happened to him. He's a bit odd, but really a good guy. The only information I recall he had, and I'm not sure I believe this, him being crazy and all, was that he saw Kimberly walking across the bridge with a little girl."

"Did Stu say if Kimberly was willingly going with this child? Were there any adults around?" Candice asked. Was this child being used as bait for an adult predator? Both the F.B.I. and Candice's own police department *had* considered this, but lacked sufficient information to form any conclusions.

"Not really believable. Just his schizophrenic, crazy imagination, if you ask me." Edgar emphasized crazy by circling his finger by the side of his head. "But, still cool. I really hope he's okay somewhere."

"Do you know anywhere else, beside the park, that Stu frequented?"

"Yeah," Edgar answered. "All the homeless sorts hang around the gas station." He pointed to a service station up the hill, and across the street from the park entrance. Candice had passed it and noticed it was boarded up and the pumps gone. She would have to check on its history. How long had it been vacant?

"How about this girl?" She showed Edgar a school picture of Rachel Stephenson.

"No, sorry. The other detective asked the same thing."

"Thanks. I know it gets old answering the same questions over and over again, but sometimes it helps the investigation to ask in person."

"Totally understand. Wish I could do more to help. I've been keeping my eye out ever since this stuff started. After work, I make a point of driving around the park."

"We appreciate that. Here's my card. Make sure you don't confront anyone. Just call." Candice handed him her card.

"Will do," Edgar replied.

So, the most promising lead was still a missing homeless man named Stu, who had fallen off the radar sometime in the year since the girls disappeared. His last known locations had been the park and gas station.

Candice drove to the station. It had once housed a mini-market as well, and she wondered why a service station in such a strategic corner would go out of business or why a new one had not arisen to take its place. The windows were boarded up and green paint was peeling from the sides of the building.

"Stu?" Candice asked a man sitting on the steps.

"Stu?" the man answered. He was dressed in an old sailor's coat, stained and torn. Beside him, sat a small dog that the man was feeding pieces of bologna.

"That's right. Are you Stu, sir?" She showed him her police credentials.

"No, I'm Tom."

"Do you know a man named Stu?" Candice asked.

"Did. Don't think it's his real name, though. Ain't seen him an ages."

"When was the last time you saw him? And where."

"Don't remember. May have been at our camp down there by the old bridge."

"When was this?"

"Goodness lady, I don't know."

"Could you make a guess? Was it summer? Winter?"

"It would have been last summer – 'bout the times those girls went missing."

"What do you know about the girls?" Candice asked.

The man looked down. "I don't know nothing I haven't heard."

"Heard from where?"

"The news. We sometimes stop in the River Coffee Shop. The manager's cool and doesn't make no fuss so long as we don't come in all at once and don't make trouble." He paused and looked down at his dog which stared at him expectantly, waiting for another piece of bologna. "They have a TV set up. Saw it on the TV, ma'am."

"I'm not worried about you being involved in this at all, okay. I just need to find Stu. He's not involved either. He just saw something we need to ask him about. He's not in any trouble and you're not in any trouble." She drew a business card from her breast pocket and handed it to him. "If you see Stu, can you give me a call? If you can't get to a phone, just flag down any police cruiser and let them know. Thank you."

The man agreed and Candice returned to her car after a quick tour around the area.

That night, she dressed in her room. She was going back to the site, but at night, a time she felt she was more likely to run into transients – perhaps even Stu himself. She exchanged her service semi-automatic for a small revolver, one easily hidden in the undercover holster around her belt, but still readily accessible. Next she grabbed the large, police flashlight she kept by her bed. At the highest setting of 220 lumens, it had sufficient candlepower to momentarily disorient anyone. She also took a pencil flashlight from her kit and put it in her pocket. She was wearing tall boots. She didn't think she would run into any snakes, but it was rattlesnake country and it would be dark. Her pants were black, of the water resistant type as was her top. She would wear a double-sided coat, white side out while in transit across the park – she didn't want to be hit by a car or bicyclist, after all – then, once there, turn it inside out to the non-reflective black part so she would be hard to see.

Chapter 18

Rachel awoke to daylight and in a bed so soft she felt nearly weightless after weeks sleeping on the hard forest floor. Gone also was the moldy, dusty smell of her sleeping bag and in its place was the scent of fine linen and pine. She was in a room, that while small, was not cramped and had a ceiling at a steep angle like an attic, but she could see through the window to the yard outside and knew she must be on the ground floor. The walls were wood and of a dark red-earth colored mahogany. The room had visible supports, but these were of quilted maple and lighter in color. The main window was low like those on a passenger ship or aircraft, but was rectangular and covered much of the bottom half of the wall. It protruded to the outside, Tudor style. At each corner stood a potted plant with flowers, flowers of pink, yellow and red of a type Rachel didn't recognize, although she judged them to be closer to the kind one found in wild fields rather than what one would purchase at a florist.

Along the wall, shelves held copper pots with pewter handles, crystal glasses and pitchers and a decanter that appeared to be made entirely of diamond. Rachel wanted to step up and examine the vase, but she did not trust her body enough yet to risk it. Besides she was a guest here, after all, and would wait until she was told to "make herself at home", before doing so.

A soft voice sang from another room:

> *Through the meadow, by the stream,*
>
> *Rushed a witch of great esteem,*
>
> *Sparkling pretties in her hand,*
>
> *Forcing us to take a stand,*
>
> *Run, little witch, run —*

Rachel sat up in the bed, knocking a cup on the nightstand over with her elbow as she struggled to pull herself up.

The singing stopped. Rachel heard little footsteps coming.

"So you are up, child-witch?" Rachel heard the voice before seeing the figure as the bed was higher than the mountain witch was tall. Rachel saw only the top of her head, a moving head of tightly braided deep brown hair.

Rachel looked down to see the face and figure of a grown woman in a body the size of a child. The outlines of her face were softer than an adult's, though several tufts of gray hair did flare out from her wooden hairpiece. Her clothing reminded Rachel of the

Shepherdess paintings by the nineteenth century French Artist William Bougereau, but this witch's dress was far more colorful, with a cream skirt, pink bodice and apron. It was closer to the Dirndl, the traditional dress of European Alpine peasants – an outfit that consisted of a bodice, blouse, full skirt and apron in separate pieces – than the Italian costumes of Bougereau's work.

"Hello, then," the witch said. She carried a silver tray with soup and a cup of tea. "My name is Eustice. This is my cottage. Welcome, child-witch."

"Hello. I'm Rachel. How did I get here?"

"Jakob carried you here."

Rachel ate her soup without speaking while Eustice sat on a stool by the bed. Midway through cleaning her bowl – and Rachel found to her surprise that she was famished – another mountain witch entered the room. This one was dressed the same as Eustice except her skirt was earth green.

"Greetings, Sister." The newly entered witch's voice had a lower pitch than either Eustice or Katie's and it lent an air of gravity to her. She also had more gray hair than Eustice.

"Greetings, Gertrude-Witch," Eustice replied.

Rachel waited to be addressed before speaking, but she smiled down at Gertrude.

"Welcome child-witch. Most blessed it is to see you stir. Welcome to our village," Gertrude said.

"Thank you. Good to meet you." Rachel mentally kicked herself for her lack of a graceful, more formal greeting to her hosts.

During the remainder of the day, many mountain witches came to greet her. Rachel established that Eustice was a seamstress and Gertrude was some sort of senior witch as well as a healer. Most brought treats for Rachel to eat and, eat she did – until she could fit no more. By mid-afternoon, her strength had partly returned, but Eustice would not let her up.

"Wait, child-witch. Let yourself heal. Your vessel has been through a big shock and it needs time to recover," Gertrude admonished her.

"Yes, you must get better! You shall get better, by the Old Oak, I swan!" Eustice added.

Rachel had no idea what that last sentence meant, but understood Eustice wished her well.

Rachel followed her instructions to rest, for despite, her amiable nature, Gertrude had a commanding air - especially on nursing matters.

Towards evening of the next day, as the sun lowered in the sky and shadows were cast more deeply, another mountain witch came to visit. "This is Agnes-Witch. She is our village novelist," Eustice said by way of introduction.

Agnes curtsied to Rachel.

Rachel returned the bow as well as she could from the bed. "Pleased to meet you, Agnes-Witch. I would love to read your work."

"Oh, dearest me, I have some of my humble works for thee!" Agnes flushed pink and reached into her bag and came out with a handful of novels that she handed to Rachel.

"Thanks." Rachel took them, but Agnes continued to pull out novels and hand them to Rachel. So many, that she had to stack them on the nightstand. By the time she was done, Agnes had given Rachel more than thirty books.

Rachel had been in the village long enough not to be surprised by a bag holding items many times its size.

She read some of the titles: *The Passionate Seamstress, The Passionate Shepherdess, The Passionate Shepherd, Love is Lost, Into the Mist, The Passion and the Fury.* Okay, Rachel thought, they have their own Barbara Cartland – the romance writer who made Harlequin Romance novels popular – and now I have to read her. This should be interesting. The mountain witches, it appeared, were incurable romantics.

At evening tea, Gertrude gave Rachel permission to make short trips out of bed and the next morning, Eustice called Rachel into the living room to show her her sewing kit. The mountain witch was standing on one of the rolling ladders she kept in her cottage and was removing a box from one of the many overhead cupboards with wood button handles in her storeroom.

The kit was carefully arranged inside a rosewood box. No, to call it simply a box would be like saying the *Hope Diamond* was just a rock. No wonder Katie had so admired Rachel's mechanical watch — these mountain witches were craftsmen of the highest order. The kit contained glittering scissors, of surgical quality, which were held down by crimson velvet bands; rows of needles that sparkled in the light, lined up by size, row by row, along the edges; pincushions and thimbles decorated with exquisite patterns; and rows of threads of every conceivable size and color.

Gertrude joined them as Rachel examined the kit.

"My dear sister, Eustice-Witch is a most excellent seamstress." Gertrude patted Rachel's arm. Behind her stood the leader of the mountain witches, Queen Erzsebet, in a dark, viridian green dress, accented by crème colored blouse and black hair. She had on the necklace, a miniature Mountain Witch village carved in what appeared to be diamond, which was the symbol of her office for all but the most formal occasions – when she wore her crown.

"We must talk now, if you are feeling up to it," Queen Erzsebet said in a pleasant tone, but Rachel knew it was as much of an order as a request. Gertrude had introduced her to Rachel the evening before during a brief visit by the queen to the cottage.

The contrast with Katie, and her extreme reserve – mysteriousness even – was extreme. These mountain witches: Gertrude, Eustice and Erzsebet, were more – and Rachel hated to admit it about her friend – forthright than Katie. More earthy, as well. True, Katie smelled of the soil and of greenery, but these witches smelled of life, of fresh carpentry, of clean linen. If Katie were Creation, these witches were Life itself. Compared to them, Katie had a metallic touch like a sensitive tooth exposed to extremes in temperature.

Her time with these witches made Rachel remember that short visits with Katie were generally pleasant – delightful, even, but, longer visits, in retrospect, tended to become unnerving. Rachel sensed an undercurrent of sterility, a vague feeling that Katie was not an organic, living creature. Silly, to think this way, but *these mountain witches were more alive.*

She took out the yellow, fire marble Katie had left her. That was her friend's way - don't present things, just leave them in Rachel's drawer for her to find. She had to take the marble; it was too fine and pretty to discard and it had the same feel of energy and power that Katie possessed. When asked about it, Katie's only response had been a cryptic "We are together, you and I."

Gertrude had pulled her rocking chair beside Eustice, who in atypical fashion, was not flittering about like a hummingbird, but sitting still with her arms folded in her lap.

"There were some people following me: a man with a dog and a tall, blonde woman in a dark blue dress. Do you know who they are and what they wanted?" Rachel asked.

"Yes. They are from the Citadel: the witch capital city of our universe. They were watching you because you possess the ability to use the Power and they want to protect you, train you how to use your Gift safely."

"Why didn't they just take me then? Kidnap me, instead of stalking me? Or, better yet, come talk to me instead of scaring me witless."

Erzsebet smiled. "It is not that easy. You are a powerful witch. A child-witch, for sure, but still powerful"

"I can't do much with it yet."

"Not consciously, but if you felt threatened or backed into a corner, you could go into the rage."

"The Rage?"

"A powerful witch who has lost conscious control over herself and her power and lashes out at anything in her way," Erzsebet replied.

"Will they come here?"

"Yes, when you are better and back on your feet. Mountain Witches are Protected Entities under the Accords and members of the Citadel and Witches Council visit frequently. The Accords are a signed treaty and agreement between magical realms."

"To take me away?"

"Only if you consent. They wish only to speak with you at this time. Their intentions are kindly. It was Jacob, from the Citadel who carried you here."

"How did you find me?"

"Your signal."

"I didn't send a signal. None that I am aware of."

Gertrude and Erzsebet looked at each other, then Erzsebet spoke, "You have some familiarity with witches and the Power. Who told you these things?"

Rachel explained her first, tentative uses of the Power and how Katie had shown up at her doorstep within days of her first conscious use of the Gift, then of the book she had given Rachel. Rachel did not mention her dream of walking throughout the Cosmos on the night she was ill.

"I have a copy of that book as well. It is called *Powers of the Realm*. You may borrow it whenever you like, and I will try to answer any questions you have," Queen Erzsebet said.

"You have a watch. I noticed a silver pocket watch in your front blouse pocket."

"Yes, a gift from my sisters upon my ascension to the throne."

"So you know about mechanical watches, then?"

"Of course. Some of our sisters make mechanical watches in this very village and are well known throughout the realm for their work. It is in high demand."

"I don't understand. Katie was fascinated by mine. She acted as if she had never seen one before, but she did know what electronic watches were and paid them no more mind than any other electronic device?"

"Perhaps she never had seen one," Queen Erzsebet answered.

"How could that be if mountain witches make them?"

"Because she is not a mountain witch. She is a sorceress. A very powerful and dangerous one."

Chapter 19

Why had Katie signaled them? Had it been her? Were they – Katie, the Citadel, and the mountain witches – working together, but unwilling to admit it? Had Katie brought Rachel into this world to trap her? Another question: how had her gear and tent gotten here as well?

A week passed before she was able to get out of bed for longer than ten-minute periods. Gertrude and Eustice were her constant companions. Queen Erzsebet visited once more. Before leaving for a Council meeting in the next village, she repeated her invitation to Rachel to enjoy the hospitality of the village and to consider it her home.

Rachel continued to stay in Eustice's cottage, though she had invitations to stay in other cottages. Agnes even offered to get Jacob to build one of her own.

"It's time to exercise. It's time to move ourselves," a chorus of mountain witches called from the village square. She had heard this before, but had been too unwell to see what was going on. Today she put down her knitting, for Eustice was teaching her the art, and went outside to see what the commotion was about.

Over a dozen witches – more than Rachel had ever seen – were gathered on the green. Seemed like nearly the entire population of the village. They grabbed hands and made a circle around her. The started slowly, then, like a multi-colored merry go round with large porcelain dolls instead of horses as the spinning rides, they whirled about her, faster and faster, stirring up clouds of fine dust. This went on for several minutes, until Rachel became dizzy and nearly toppled over. Fortunately, they slowed just as she felt herself beginning to get seasick.

"Center!" Agnes called.

All eyes were upon Rachel. What did they want her to do?

Gertrude stepped forward beside Rachel. "Follow with me and do as I do, dear child." Gertrude took a shoulder-width stance and raised her arms toward the skies. "It is a great honor to be an exercise leader, and we welcome you to our circle to lead us in our strenuations."

Strenuations? Now what on earth were those? Gertrude twirled her arms, making circles in the air above her head. She then began a series of arm exercises that Rachel attempted to follow, but could not keep up with. Good grief, these witches do aerobics. She would only be mildly surprised at this point to see them wheel out a large flat-screen television with DVD player, and exercise videos.

Rachel was breathing heavily after the exercise ended. She had recovered her balance and most of her strength, but regaining her wind would take some time and exercise.

Millie came up to her, panting. "A most agreeable showing."

"Fine performance, child-witch. Thee definitely has a gift for it!" Agnes added, and curtsied to Rachel.

The mountain witches gathered around her. One by one, they congratulated her on serving as exercise leader – a position she hadn't realized was hers. She flushed and thanked them. "It was an honor. Perhaps next time I will do better."

"All of us have to learn the first time, "Eustice said.

"Certainly, we did. It takes time to become accustomed to our ways." Gertrude took Rachel's hand. "Come, it is time to introduce you to our friends."

Rachel put her hand to her head, twirled a lock of hair, then asked, "From the Witches Council? The Citadel?" These kind, little witches surely did not intend her harm, but she had thought the same of Katie once.

No, Katie always had her secrets. She would trust these witches.

"Yes, our most dear friends, Karen and Jakob. They are waiting for you inside." Eustice took Rachel's other hand.

The two representatives were seated inside Gertrude's cottage. Rachel recognized them immediately: the Blue Dress Woman from the church parking lot, and the man walking his dog in the Stephenson's neighborhood. They did not speak as she entered.

Rachel stopped at the doorway, hesitant to enter. These were the folks who had so terrified her.

"Do not worry, child-witch. They mean you no harm and will explain everything." Eustice took Rachel's arm and led her inside.

"Please, Rachel, sit down." Gertrude motioned to a wicker chair by the wall. "These two are Representatives of the Witches' Council. They believe you to be in very great peril. Peril from that powerful sorceress and peril from your own strong, but untrained and undisciplined abilities."

"Hello." Rachel took a seat. She wondered if Gertrude had rehearsed her introduction of the two representatives.

Jakob smiled, rose, and offered her his hand. She took it.

Karen stood next to him, and patted Rachel's shoulder. "We are so happy to see you well. We were so worried about you."

"Gertrude said you carried me from my tent to here. Thank you." Rachel said.

"Glad to have done it," Jakob said.

They all took their seats and Karen began, "Do not be frightened of us. We were only following you for your safety. It was necessary for your own protection."

They were both sitting up straight with their feet flat on the floor. Rachel recognized the intense discipline in both of them – an erect self-confidence shared by elite soldiers; tenured Ivy League Professors, certain of their standing and personal accomplishment; of chief residents in large hospitals; of ship's captains. Jakob wore a light brown flannel shirt carefully tucked into his slacks, Karen wore a blue-green dress, different and less formal than the one Rachel had seen her wearing at the church, but still with a vest and high collar. The emerald in the brooch she wore at her collar reflected the ambient light in the room. Rachel couldn't help staring at it for a moment.

"There was a Possessor following me after church. Did you get it away from me?" Rachel asked.

"Yes. Jakob dealt with it," Karen said.

"Thank you. I didn't know what to do."

"We couldn't talk to you, because Katie blocked us from getting close. Also, you might have turned your own strength upon us, perhaps even gone into the Rage, if you felt your little friend was endangered by us."

"But you were at the church. Why didn't you approach me then? All you did was scare the life out of me."

"Katie put a field around you that prevented us from doing so. It was not until you left your world that the field was broken," Karen said.

"I understand that. But why did you follow me the way you did instead of remaining hidden?" Rachel said.

"That was Katie's doing. She prevented us from shielding ourselves from your view. The only alternative to following you the way we did was to abandon you to her. That we were not willing to do," Jakob said.

"So, Katie wanted me to be afraid of you?" Rachel asked.

"She found it useful for you to be," Jakob said.

"What do you know about her?" Rachel asked.

"We have been tracking her for years. You are the fifth child-witch this sorceress has befriended. She finds them when they first begin to channel, as you did, and discards them if they are not suitable for her purpose. You are the first she has attempted to keep," Karen answered.

"Is she evil? What does she want with me?"

"As to your first question, no, she is not evil, but she is not socialized into human values and behaviors. If she wants something, she takes it, without regard to the consequences to others."

"We saw your tent was full of books. You obviously read a lot. Have you ever heard of Friedrich Nietzsche?" Jakob asked.

"The philosopher?" Rachel asked.

"Yes. He was a German philosopher of the 1800's." Karen said.

"I have heard of him but I'm not familiar with his works," Rachel answered.

"When Katie was first starting out in this world, while still very young, and unguided, she read his works. He wrote of an Overman, a Superman, a being that transcended human limitations and actualized the unrealized potential of man. She took this idea and ran with it and, given the amount of power she has, her lack of restraint makes her dangerous."

"Is she human?"

"She was, but is no longer."

"She wants my power? Why? If she can do so many things, why would she want someone like me?" Rachel asked.

"Katie is a sorceress and can manipulate reality at the quantum level, but she has a limited ability to store power. She needs a witch, preferably a young, unsettled one, to channel power for her," Karen said.

"What would she do with the Power?"

"Explore," Jakob said. "Katie is still very much a child. A powerful one, yes, filled with knowledge and intelligence, but with impulses that are still those of a child exploring its world, oblivious to the consequences of her behavior to others or the world around her."

"How is this exploring bad?"

"Because of what she could do to the fabric of the cosmos with her manipulations," Karen said.

"And because of the harm she could do to you, and others like you." Jakob looked protectively at Rachel.

"She believes in Nietzsche's Superman, because, well, according to her, …she's it," Karen said.

"And her understanding, even of that, is superficial. She does not understand moral limits and has never been fully socialized into human society – not any other," Jakob said.

"What do we do?" Rachel asked.

"You stay here. The longer you are away from Katie, the older you get and the more experienced you become in the Power, the less hold she can have over you. She can only use you while you are young and pliable," Karen said.

"Time is on your side, not hers," Jakob added.

"So that's why she wouldn't answer my questions or show me how to protect myself with the Power."

"There is that, but also, as a sorceress, she doesn't use power in the same way you do. Witches channel energy through them. Sorceresses and sorcerers manipulate the world by using the power around them. That power can include any witch in the area."

"Do you have any more questions for us?" Karen asked.

"I do not understand this world. So many things you do are different from what they are in my world, on Earth, and some things are nearly identical," Rachel said.

"There are many worlds, many universes, and many kingdoms within each. Yours and ours are connected. In fact, many of our people started out in your world, and brought their language and traditions here with them."

She looked around the cottage, and Rachel understood her to mean that this was the case with the mountain witches. "It's complex. You will understand it better after some time here."

"Will I go back to my own world?"

"When you are ready, you may be able to, if you so wish, but you may not want to after you have been here long enough."

"I never contacted my family. I meant to do that."

"We are working on that. Steps are being taken by one of our sisters here to bring closure to your world."

"Okay. Why are some things the same, and others so different? Katie was a witch...well a sorceress, yet she used a cell phone to send me text messages. She even bought me my own phone."

"We pick from among those innovations and technologies that can serve us without becoming our masters," Getrude said.

"Katie uses whatever suits her, or piques her fancy. She may select some technological item because it interests her to do so, not because she necessarily needs it," Karen said.

"We are closer geographically than people in your world. We have no need of such devices and we like our peace and quiet," Eustice said.

"I've seen several muskets in cottages I've visited. Are they for self-defense? If so, why muskets and not machineguns?" Rachel asked.

"We have them to defend against malicious creatures such as Grabbers; although, one of those hasn't invaded our mountain in a generation. We don't use modern firearms because each round needs to be guided separately to its target by the Power. Otherwise, anyone with the Gift can deflect it."

"Why not use modern cartridge rifles then? Just shoot one round at a time?"

"Because muzzle loading rifles and muskets allow us to vary the amount and type of powder used with every shot."

"So did the Gift just appear in me this year, or have I always had it without knowing it?"

"It has always been there."

"But I only just used it, like six or seven months ago," Rachel said.

"Your first *conscious* use may have been only in the past year, but think about it. How many children have survived the sort of childhood you had? How many flourished and landed on their feet, as you have?"

"I have wondered that," Rachel said. "So many times I was close to being killed, yet survived."

"As a young witch hits puberty, the Gift strengthens and becomes more active. This stage varies from witch to witch. Some have their first conscious manifestation of the Power at as young as nine or ten years old; some don't until their middle twenties," Karen said.

Chapter 20

The thimble hovered over the table as Rachel willed it to levitate.

"You are learning very quickly, Rachel," Karen said at the close of an afternoon lesson in the use of the Power. They were inside Eustice's cottage and knitting lay on the bed. "Tomorrow morning, Jakob and I must leave on important business for the Citadel."

Rachel looked up from her work. She studied under Karen every morning and afternoon. In these lessons, Rachel learned how to use the Gift to increase intuition and mental focus, along with general principles of magic and basic skills such as lighting a candle with the Power and manipulating fine objects such as a needle and thread.

"Do not worry, " Karen continued. "Gertrude-Witch will continue your lessons."

Gertrude proved to be an excellent teacher, as well. Different from Karen, but effective in her own way. From her, Rachel learned how to sense life around her; how to know a deer, or other animal is close in the forest. Various other mountain witches worked with her on crafts, using both manual skills and the Power to fashion ornaments, utensils, and simple cloth items such as handkerchiefs tablecloths. Others showed her how they made their houses, from laying the foundation to selecting what they referred to as the most "sparkling" of wood for the interior.

One evening, after six days of busy, exhausting, but rewarding work, Gertrude came to her and said, "Rachel, you are now ready to go on an outing with the Upper Mountain Witches. This expedition will bring together much of what you have been working on here, with us, and allow you to meet our elder sister among the Upper Mountain Witches, Queen Annalisse."

"What are Upper Mountain Witches?"

"There are Upper Mountain Witches and there are and Lower Mountain Witches. We are Lower Mountain Witches and Erzsebet is our Queen. Annalisse is Queen of the Upper Mountain Witches. We Lower Mountain witches live in villages in the foothills and valleys, the Upper Mountain Witches are nomadic and live in the heights."

They started out the next morning, Gertrude, Eustice and Rachel, directly after first light. Mist blanketed the valley floor and obscured the mountains ahead; the daisies and geraniums had dew upon their petals, leaves and stems.

At the edge of the village, Eustice knocked at one of the cottages. The door opened and Agnes stepped out, satchel over her shoulder.

"Dearest me! Thee shall seek that which dwells in yonder hills!" Agnes curtsied to Rachel.

Rachel returned the bow. Was the witch bringing some of her romance novels with her?

Once they left the boundary of the village, Rachel could barely see ahead, but Gertrude knew the way and they made good progress. Sometime after crossing the field beyond the mountain witch village, they reached the shallow creek separating the valley from the mountains. Rachel knew that if they were to follow the creek, they would have to do so from the leeward side of the mountain – unless they were actually going to enter the Kingdom of the Upper Mountain Witches – for the creek marked the boundary between the two territories.

To her surprise, they followed the creek until it split into two parts. One continued its path around the foothills and the other rose into the mountains. They followed the section that rose: a tributary of the main river that crossed the peaks and brought the snow melt to the valley lake below.

At the foot of the first peak, the party stopped.

"We must wait here for the queen," Gertrude said.

Agnes sat down on one of the many boulders that lined the river at this point. Eustice sat beside her and Rachel joined them.

Agnes removed a jar of apricot jam and loaf of bread from her satchel and began tearing off pieces of bread and spooning jam on them. The bread was still warm and steam rose from it. The scent of newly baked bread reminded Rachel that she was hungry. Eustice took several cups from Agnes's satchel and filled them with water from the stream and passed them out.

For several minutes, they waited and Gertrude finally joined them, taking a seat on the rock between Eustice and Rachel. After they had their fill, Agnes returned the remainder of the loaf to her satchel.

Through the mist, Rachel saw a figure emerge. Its silhouette was too obscured by mist and distance to distinguish, but it was too small to be a deer.

Gertrude rose from her place on the rock, followed by Eustice then Agnes and, finally, Rachel. None spoke. Rachel stroked the side of her skirt with her fingers.

The shape approached them, and as the distance closed, Rachel could make out the figure of a small woman. She was taller than the mountain witches in Gertrude's party, but still much shorter than Rachel herself and carried an ancient looking rifle. As the figure came within a few yards of their party, Rachel saw that the woman was not alone. Behind her three others, though slightly shorter, walked behind, so silently they could have passed for ghosts. Rachel took the tall one to be the leader as the other three Upper Mountain Witches stopped behind her, at a respectful distance, gazes directed at the tallest, as if waiting for her cue. All three were dressed ruggedly, with coats of dull earth colors and wool leggings under short skirts of burlap.

Eustice curtsied to the leader. The others in her party did likewise. Rachel followed their lead and gave the strange looking group the best curtsy she could muster, taking her cue from the others, and from memories of movies with royalty in them.

"Queen Annalisse," Eustice said, "thank you for your great kindness in offering to guide this child-witch up your mountain."

Annalisse's gray cloak called to mind images from black and white pictures of Confederate soldiers during the American Civil War. Over Queen Annalisse's golden brown hair, she wore a cavalier's hat, of the style seen in the Dutch artist Vermeer's paintings from the 1600's. Her blouse, which peeked through the separation in the front of the cloak, was antique white; the collar held together by a copper pin. The pin carried an insignia, but Rachel could not make it out.

At approximately three feet, nine inches, Annalisse was by far the tallest mountain witch Rachel had ever seen. Hadn't Gertrude said that Upper Mountain Witches selected their queen by height? Given what Rachel knew about historic royalty in her native Romania as well as the rest of Europe, she had thought choosing a monarch by height was as good a way as any.

"It is an honor to meet you, Queen Annalisse." Rachel curtsied again.

Annalisse nodded. She smelled faintly of subalpine flora such as whitebark pine, juniper, and mountain daisies, but this was somewhat overpowered by the scent of damp wool from her leggings.

"So, where are we going, Eustice-Witch?" Rachel whispered as they made their way up the hill.

"Soon enough, you will see, dear child," Eustice answered.

After a moment, Gertrude spoke, "This is to show you how to channel undetected, Rachel. You may need this skill someday. Queen Annalisse will guide us because this is her territory, and because she is the most skilled at this among the mountain witches, Upper or Lower."

Queen Annalisse drew a candle from her satchel and set in on the rock in front of Rachel. The antique pewter candle holder reflected little of the morning light. Along the top of the candle, drops of dried wax roughened the surface.

Annalisse turned to Gertrude.

"This candle flame will rise or fall as you channel. The more power you allow to escape, the higher the flame will rise on the candle. You must shield yourself from sending up a signal every time you channel. Focus on the task at hand, and try to allow only the item you are affecting to receive the power," Gertrude said.

"The better you get at this, the better protected you will be from that sorceress!" Eustice said.

"Hush, now, Eustice-Witch," Gertrude said. "Today, Queen Annalisse is going to allow you to stalk one of her mountain goats. These creatures can sense the Power, and you will have to train yourself not to bleed off power or the animal will bolt. It may even attack if it feels provoked."

"Goats?" Rachel asked.

"Yes. These mountain goats are fierce and strong. Utterly untamable. They weigh up to three hundred pounds and have two horns with which they can make powerful, deadly thrusts. Now we must continue, and quietly, Annalisse has instructed," Gertrude said.

Eustice handed the candle to Rachel and instructed her to hold it upright in her hand when they got to their destination. Rachel put the candle in her apron pocket and the party started up the mountain. The climb was not difficult at first as they followed a well-worn trail used by both Upper and Lower witches as well as traders and visitors from the Citadel.

When Annalisse, disappeared into the bush, the troupe left the main path.

Rachel slowed, wondering how the Upper Mountain Witch queen had vanished so abruptly, but Gertrude and Eustice hurried her on. She picked her pace back up and followed Agnes into the brush, putting a hand in front of her face, expecting to meet branches and pine needles, but was surprised to find a clear path opened before her. The impenetrable brush concealed an Upper Mountain Witch trail up the steep side of the mountain.

The trail was only wide enough for the party to go single file. Gertrude went before her; Eustice and Agnes followed. From time to time, Rachel saw the top of Annalisse's cavalier hat as they rounded corners.

The rich, deep foliage, with its many shades of green, gave way to rocky, uneven terrain sparsely populated by weeds, moss and juniper – with only the infrequent whitebark pine or mountain hemlock projecting form the ledges. Still, the mountain smelled of evergreen. Rachel kept as close as possible to the side of the rock and away from the edge of the path, which now ended in a steep drop to the forest below. The only sound was the occasional pebble falling when she disturbed it. The air was colder here and she shivered beneath her sweater, the sweat from the exertion adding to her chill.

After what seemed like hours, the path ended on a promontory. She took her breath. The view across the mountain was stunning. The trees below were toy size and the river reflected the early morning light in luminous points. Annalisse stood beside her. She had neither seen nor felt the witch move.

Now, you may take the candle out and light it. Remember; you must learn to channel without making those with the Gift around you aware of it. The flame should not rise, or you are bleeding off power and sending a signal to all that you are channeling. Annalisse spoke directly into Rachel's mind.

She motioned for Rachel to raise the lighted candle. The queen then turned to the ground ahead of them. A pebble moved. There was a nearly imperceptible flicker of the candle. Annalisse turned back to Rachel and the girl understood Annalisse wished her to do the same, to use the Power to move an object while minimizing leakage.

Rachel located a group of pebbles at the end of the rock shelf they stood on and fixed upon one of them. She braced her body against the side of the mountain and cleared her mind of all concerns, past and present, and willed the pebble to move. It flew off the mountain and the candle flame flared up, warming her face. Okay, not so good.

Annalisse put her left hand over her own abdomen and slowly breathed in through her nose, and motioned with her hand how the breath was filling her abdomen. After a long breath, she exhaled slowly through her mouth. She repeated this, then pointed at Rachel to try.

Imitating Queen Annalisse as best she could, Rachel inhaled through her nose. She took too much air in the first attempt and had to start over. In slowing the process to take as long as Annalisse, she found herself holding her breath and tensing for a moment before beginning her exhalation. This also came too quickly. Annalisse motioned for her to try again. This time she did far better, anticipating her lungs filling up and breathing in with a slower, more measured movement. She still had a pause between inhaling and exhaling, but it was much shorter and did not cause her dizziness. The queen had her repeat the exercise until Rachel had enough smoothness to her technique that she felt herself calm and her head clear.

When she again tried the exercise with the candle, the flame rose, but only half as high as the first time. She tried again, same result. Annalisse signalled to her to breathe before her next attempt, and this time the rock flew, but the candle flickered only for an instant. They continued the exercise until Rachel was half-exhausted from the concentration.

"Let us see how it works when you are presented with a threat. We will hike a ways further and try this exercise in the presence of a mountain goat. If it feels you channeling his way, he will charge," Queen Annalissse said.

It will charge? In only an hour, Rachel had more than quadrupled her ability to channel safely, but could she do so under stress? This lesson from Annalisse was how she imagined a class with a martial arts master would be.

They hiked further up the mountain. The exertion from pushing away branches that hung from the handful of tree-like bushes and blocked Rachel's way; the effort required to navigate the path in the areas where erosion and beds of small rock made it irregular, and the sparser air at the higher altitude, all pushed Rachel's stamina to the limit. By the time Annalisse instructed them to stop, Rachel was breathing heavily and half-collapsed against the stone side of the peak they had ascended.

Annalisse looking at something along the edge of the path, but Rachel was too tired at the moment to care. The queen said something to Gertrude and, after a moment, Gertrude approached Rachel. "We are here. Queen Annalisse has found a buck for you."

Rachel willed herself to her feet. She was tall enough to see over the rocks and foliage that edged the path, but did not see a goat. She turned to the queen. "I don't see anything."

Annalisse pointed towards a crag on the peak opposite them.

Rachel strained to see. "I'm sorry, where is it?"

"Rachel, don't look for movement, it is standing still. Look for the horns," Gertrude said.

Rachel scanned the peak again. The pattern on one of the boulders was curved and she stared at this. Like one of those optical illusions that only becomes clear after a moment of concentration, she made out the shape of the buck below the curls in the rock. The curls were not a pattern on the rock face, they were the goat's horns. "How do we get there? Do we have to get closer?"

Annalisse did not answer, but instead climbed over the side of the path. The other witches followed. Rachel crouched to lower her profile and stepped over the side of the path after them. And nearly fell.

The witches had descended into another, deeper path, and Rachel, expecting only the distance of a single step down, found herself plunging two feet. She wanted to stop and collect herself, but the witches were already far ahead and she had to hurry to catch up to them. If the path had allowed it, she would have run. How was she supposed to learn if they were doing this?

Rachel caught up with the party. After descending, the trail ran level for hundreds of yards before rising towards the peak opposite the one from where they had just come. She couldn't see the point of this; they wouldn't have to channel to spook the goat – the commotion she made headed in its direction would be enough to arouse it. Just as she thought this, the witches turned to the left and disappeared. Irritated, Rachel followed, and again nearly fell once more as the path dropped. What use is this if I break my ankle?

Eventually, she caught up to them where they were gathered behind a boulder. Annalisse was peeking behind it and waved Rachel closer. Rachel took a second to get her breath first. When she did, she saw a goat the size of a horse with two, scythe-like horns, protruding from its forehead.

"You will go forward, with Queen Annalisse. Follow her lead and do what she asks of you, no matter how uncomfortable or frightened you may be," Gertrude whispered and pushed Rachel forward.

Rachel nearly stumbled as she followed the fast moving queen off the path where they flanked the goat. By the time it again came in view, it lay on the crag, staring warily out across the valley between the two peaks, its cream-colored fur peppered with streaks of gray ranging from light, to nearly coal black. But they were close enough that it did not camouflage the goat as effectively as it had from a distance. The mountain path was steep from the crag to where Rachel and Annalisse crouched. There were now no obstructions between them and the beast to protect them should it charge. Rachel could smell the musk scent of the creature, though they were upwind from it, and could see the steam rising from its mouth as it exhaled into the cold mountain air.

Queen Annalisse turned in the opposite direction of the goat and pointed to the branch of a wiry bush growing into the side of the cliff, its bundles of needles just visible. When she was sure Rachel was watching, Annalisse channeled, causing the needles of the branch to flutter, as if struck by a rogue, funnel wind. When she stopped, Rachel moved forward, prepared to take her place, but the witch stood her ground and took Rachel's hand. Annalisse's grip was soft as velvet, yet secure as iron. After Rachel had adjusted to her spot, Annalisse nodded to her and Rachel understood what was expected.

With a dangerous and wary beast behind her, one atuned to the slightest gasp of the Power, Rachel was tense to near fright. Annalisse faced Rachel and breathed as during the morning's exercises. Rachel did the same, but it took many breaths to be calm enough to focus on the branch and not the threat behind them. Finally,

Annalisse motioned her to channel and move the branch. Rachel prepared to comply and moved her hands to her front, but Annalisse held firm to her right hand. Rachel cleared her mind and breathed in slowly one final time. As she exhaled the final portion of her breath, she channeled. Her arm rose and then the branch swayed.

Why had her hand risen? She had not moved it of her own volition, and why had Queen Annalisse insisted on holding her hand? Rachel looked questioningly at the witch who simply motioned towards the branch for a second try. She would not let Rachel turn to see if the goat was roused. Rachel guessed the mountain creature could move steathily through its range and had to trust Annalisse would give warning if this happened. The witch must have some survival alarm mechanism that didn't require active channeling or she would not have turned her back on such a dangerous creature.

Rachel breathed deeply and prepared for a second try. This time her hand moved, as the branch did, but not so much, and she realized the queen was holding her hand to prevent excess power from bleeding out and rousing the goat. They did this several more times until Rachel was focused well enough that her arm did not raise. Annalisse let go as Rachel began another attempt. The drop in tension disconcerted her and she lost her focus. The branch moved wildly, nearly detaching its needles.

Rachel felt, rather than saw – for the movement was too quick for her eyes – Annalisse turn and move behind her. It took a second for Rachel to react, herself, and turn to face the path. At the top the goat stood, staring down at Rachel, its hooves marking the ground as it prepared to charge. Time slowed for Rachel – as it had for her while in the back seat of her parents car when another driver had run a red light and totaled the Stephenson's car.

Annalisse moved towards the beast as it charged Rachel, horns lowered. At the last few feet before reaching them, it halted. Queen Annalisse said something to it in a language Rachel didn't understand, and curtsied to the goat, her musket abandoned on the path behind her. Rachel had not seen her set it down.

The goat stared for a moment at Rachel, then at Annalisse. As it turned its gaze to the queen, its amber eyes blazing, it kicked its front hoof up and down, like a bull preparing to charge a matador. Annalisse did not flinch or yield. After an interminable moment, the beast elevated its head so that its horns were no longer pointed towards the two and raised its front hoof, and lowered its body a few inches in what Rachel felt certain was its form of bowing, of demonstrating mutual respect between itself and the queen. The goat turned and was off down the side of the mountain away from them so quickly that Rachel barely saw it move.

"Thank you," Rachel mumbled. "I froze."

"It is a thing, expected, the first time out."

Rachel turned to face the voice. Above her head, carrying a spear, crouched one of the queen's Upper Mountain Witches.

Rachel bowed, her knees still shaking. "You have been up there the whole time? I did not see you."

"We are not meant to be seen." The mountain witch put out her hand. "I am Trudy-Witch."

"Rachel Stephenson." Rachel took Trudy's hand. The grip was firm, though the tiny palm cold.

Trudy smiled, then dropped down from her perch, disassembled her spear, putting the sharpened head into a burlap pouch inside her skirt. The three pieces of the staff, unhooked by some mechanism, went into a pocket on her leggings.

"Let us go now, and leave this noble beast in peace," Queen Annalisse said.

Rachel turned to the queen and nodded. When she turned back to Trudy, the witch was gone, once again invisible.

The climb down the mountain was much easier than the way up and Rachel was now familiar with the terrain enough to make her way more efficiently. Also the adrenaline dump from the near-attack numbed her to the fatigue from the hike.

The party halted before they reached the point they had met up with Queen Annalisse and her Upper Mountain Witches that morning. Gertrude told Rachel that Annalisse and her witches would take their leave now.

Rachel curtsied to Annalisse. "Thank you Queen Annalisse for guiding me today. I appreciate your efforts. And thank you for standing between me and that creature."

Annalisse returned the curtsie, but with a lesser one. She did not smile, but said, "Take care, child-witch, to remember the lessons of this morning. The time may come when you will have to channel undiscovered. Much may depend upon your doing this. Keep the candle and practice as often as you can."

It had been a productive day, but Rachel was too wound up and tired to reflect upon the lessons learned. Her final lack of effectiveness was frustrating; it had taken diminished her good nature. Still, they had done this for her and she was grateful for their effort.

Chapter 21

Aweek after their expedition with Queen Annalisse, Gertrude Witch came to her in her room as she was reading and announced, "We are going to have a Witch Got Better party for you!"

"A Witch Got Better party? What is that?" Rachel asked.

"It is our tradition to have a celebration whenever a sister recovers from a serious illness or injury. Is there anyone you would like to invite?"

"I don't know anybody in this world besides the witches in the village and I'd love all of them to be there."

"Good, they will all be very pleased to be invited. Would you mind if Leroy and Sophie come?"

"Leroy? Is he a sorcerer?"

"Oh, goodness no, dear, he's a black bear. Every mountain village needs a bear and he's ours." Gertrude laughed.

"Is he friendly?"

"Very. Sometimes a bit too friendly. He's excitable, but we'll make sure he's on his best behavior."

"Is Sophie a witch, a mountain witch?"

"Sophie, a witch?" Gertrude grinned. "She's our mountain lion. Every mountain village needs a mountain lion."

"Is she tame?"

"No, of course not. We would not do that to such a noble creature – but she is intelligent." Gertrude faced the window and pointed to the forested hills to the left of the village. "That is her territory. She often visits with our Upper Mountain Witch sisters further in the hills. She will not seek to harm you, but she is not a creature that it is wise to provoke." Gertrude said this last with a schoolmistresses nod upward. "She has a special friendship with Queen Annalisse, although she is our village's cougar."

"Also, you must invite Queen Annalisse."

"Of course. I forgot about her." Rachel said.

"Excellent," Gertrude said then looked down at her apron. A second later she viewed Rachel and said, "It is good you do, even if she chooses not to accept the invitation. It would be a grave slight not to and we must not have trouble on this mountain again. Her Upper Mountain sisters should be included, as well."

"Of course, she's invited, Gertrude. Invite anyone you think should come."

For the next few days they were busy decorating the village, hanging lamps and preparing exhibits and booths. To mountain witches, a party meant rock throwing contests, archery and musketry competitions, craft fairs, baking contests, and events such as "the Doodle" and the "Sparkling" that Rachel had no idea what they were – even after Gertrude tried to describe them to her.

The morning two days before the party, Gertrude and Eustice called to Rachel from their treehouse as she walked underneath. At first, Rachel could not tell where the voices came from. "Hello?" She answered in return.

"Up here," Eustice said and Rachel looked up to see a white bonnet peeking out of a deck built into the tree limbs. The house was constructed where the trunk branched out into the lower limbs of the tree. A deck surrounded a single room, painted light blue on the outside, but difficult to see for the branches. A pink window box protruded from the front window. To the right, a red-orange breasted robin, was building a nest in the tree, caroling as it labored.

"Oh, hello," Rachel said.

"Come on up!" Gertrude called. Rachel could not see her, so she assumed the mountain witch was inside the house. Rachel put a foot on the bottom rung of ladder. The treehouse was well crafted – not unlike the cottages in the village. The ladder, however, was made of unfinished branches lashed together and she hesitated before putting her full weight on the first rung. They were made for mountain witches, not for people.

"The ladder will hold you." Gertrude peeked out from the railing to where the ladder ascended. "We have many visitors and we have instructed our furnishings to hold the proper weights as necessary."

Rachel wondered what they meant by instructing their furnishings, but chose to hold the question for another time.

"Okay." Rachel ascended – but did so slowly and held onto the sides of the fence so that if a rung broke, she would not fall.

The walkway around the house was cramped for her, but she made it to the doorway and entered through the low doorway. Inside, Eustice was holding a red pin cushion fashioned after an apple. Yarns and pieces of cloth were draped around her neck. That's right, Rachel remembered, Eustice is a seamstress. Next to the mountain witch, and towering over her, was a mannequin the size of Rachel herself. Covering it was a dark, viridian green skirt and white blouse trimmed with intricate lace and ornamented by a crimson bow and scarf. They had made her a new outfit.

"Upper Mountain Witches always win the rock throwing contest, Eustice," Gertrude said from the corner of the room, apparently continuing a conversation from before Rachel's arrival.

"Not always! Remember when Millie-Witch won four worlds ago? She *was* a Lower Mountain Witch," Eustice answered.

"You must try this on, now, Rachel, to see if it fits," Eustice set down the pincushion and picked up a tape measure.

Fit it did –perfectly – as Rachel had never had an outfit fit. It felt both fine and comfortable on her and from the mirror in the corner, she could see that the colors set her features off just right.

"I don't know what to say," Rachel said, "You have been so kind to me."

"Wait." Gertrude produced a package from her apron and handed it to Rachel.

"What is this?" Rachel asked.

"Open it," Eustice said.

It was a light green and blue presentation box with a bow on the top half. She lifted the lid and was astonished to see a hand-hammered silver chain. Suspended from it was the largest emerald she had ever seen. Rachel no longer regretted forgetting her synthetic, green gem at the Stephenson's house, because now she had a real one of her own.

Chapter 22

From Rachel's perch in the treehouse, she could see chips in one of the nearby pillars on the village green. The witches used the structures to hold lamps during the night, or to use as signals during times of distress. There were impact indentations throughout with parts along the edges completely chipped off. She could not think what could have caused such a thing.

"I keep meaning to ask. Do you know what those dings on the pillars are from?" Rachel asked.

"Those are from the Great Mountain Witch War," Gertrude answered.

Eustice paused in her work and nodded solemnly.

"The Great Mountain Witch War? What was that? When was that?" Rachel asked.

Eustice spoke up, "It was a terrible, terrible war between the Lower Mountain Witches and the Upper Mountain Witches."

"I see." Rachel wondered what could possibly have compelled these peaceful little witches into war.

"It was a sad affair." Gertrude set down her scissors and nodded.

"What did you fight over?"

"Pull up a chair Rachel," Eustice said. "It is best for you to find out here, privately, rather than asking questions later."

"Questions which could offend," Gertrude warned. "The War of the Upper and Lower Mountain Witches was a great conflict over moissanite."

"What in the world is moissanite?"

"Moissanite is the Great Pretty." Eustice fished into her blouse and retrieved a silver, box-shaped, locket, unclasped it and handed the box to Rachel. "Open this."

Rachel tried to lift the top, but it wouldn't open at the seam. Maybe it went the other way. She turned it, but still it would not open.

"Eustice, you need to open it for the child," Gertrude said.

Eustice walked over to Rachel, squeezed the cube at the sides. It popped open. "That is the strangest box I have ever seen," Rachel said.

Inside, carved in what Rachel took to be diamond, was a sculpture of a cottage, nearly identical to Eustice's own.

"This is moissanite?" Rachel asked. "It looks like diamond."

"True," Gertrude-Witch answered, "but it sparkles brighter. During the Great Jackpot, at a time of the remotest antiquity, deposits of moissanite descended from the stars upon the land of the Mountain Witches, burying themselves for us to later find and fashion our pretties from."

That evening, Rachel looked up moissanite in her geology book, grateful that Jacob had been kind enough to retrieve her books from her camp. She took one of the candles from the shelf by the window, lit it and sat beside the small table Gertrude had brought for her to use as a desk. The mountain witch candles gave out a prodigious amount of light. Eustice, Gertrude, and presumably the other mountain witches as well, could vary the amount of light from each candle simply by touching it. That was a trick Rachel had not yet learned, so Eustice had set the candlepower to reading level. From her geology book, she read:

> Mineral moissanite was discovered by
> Henri Moissan while examining rock
> samples from a meteor crater located in
> Canyon Diablo, Arizona, in 1893. It was
> not until 1904 that he identified the
> crystals as silicon carbide, and not
> diamond, as he had first thought. This

185

mineral form of silicon carbide was
eventually named moissanite in honor of
Moissan.

Moissanite, in its natural form, is very rare
and has only been found in a small
number of places, from upper mantle rock
to meteorites. All applications of silicon
carbide today use synthetic material, as the
natural material is very scarce. Moissanite
is one of the hardest substances known,
with a hardness rating only slightly below
that of diamond, itself, making it suitable
for industrial uses where the cost of
diamond would be prohibitive.

Since 1998, when the first moissanite
reached the jewelry market, it has been
regarded as a fine gem, with optical
properties exceeding those of diamond.
Because it has its own unique appearance,
it cannot be truly called a diamond
simulant.

So, the Mountain Witches were intrigued by this
diamond substitute found largely in meteorites. So that
was the "great bonanza" – the area now the Mountain
Witch Kingdom was once bombarded with meteorites
containing moissanite. Rachel had to admit the stuff was
pretty, and she couldn't tell the difference from

diamond. In the light, it did sparkle brightly with color: blues, pinks, greens, yellows and reds.

The next day, as Gertrude, with Eustice assisting, continued her fitting for Rachel's dress, she resumed the story. "Queen Alarica the Brave, of the Upper Mountain Witches, sacked our village and made off with My great-great-great grandmother's sewing machine."

"They did. It was returned under treaty, though, Gertrude," Eustice said.

"Yes, we got the sewing machine back, but we had to give them our brass cannon. That was a pretty cannon. I've seen drawings of it."

"Who won?" Rachel asked.

"They did, at first, but we did, ultimately," Gertrude answered. "They controlled the upper mountains and knew the terrain well and how to use it in battle. They would lie in wait behind boulders and ambush our sisters with stones and darts."

"Those cursed darts," Eustice said, as if speaking from personal memory.

"How did you turn things around?" Rachel asked.

"We drew them out in the open with our pretties. First we cleared the surrounding area of boulders, trees and other places of cover, then we gathered as many of our pretties together as we could find and brought them into the center of the meadow. We knew they would not be able to resist such bait," Gertrude answered.

"All our pretties in one place, Lucinda risked all on this," Eustice said.

"Her strategy brought them out into the open and we were able to net over a dozen of them that day," Gertrude said.

"You killed a dozen of them?" Rachel asked.

"Kill our sisters?" Eustice asked, half rising out of her seat. "Of course not. How could you think such a thing of us?" They were now both gazing at Rachel.

"Uh, sorry, of course not. Of course I wouldn't think that of you. It was a stupid question, sorry." Rachel paused for a moment before continuing, "What do you mean by netting them, then?"

"The nets…" Gertrude motioned her hand to the back wall that was covered in netting of the type a deep sea fishing vessel would cast. "We caught them in our nets and took them captive."

"To the great shame of our people." Eustice nodded and looked down. Both were silent.

"How was it your shame? Didn't you win because of it?"

"Yes, but that was when Lucinda ordered the cannon to be loaded with an Upper Mountain Witch and fired at her retreating sisters."

"Lucinda paid a price for that treachery!" Eustice said.

"Not an unjust one either, sister," Gertrude answered.

"The Upper Mountain witches had been the superior fighters, even we have to admit that," Gertrude said and Eustice nodded agreement, "but we Lower Witches outnumbered them by at least three to one. Perhaps more. You see, the Upper Mountain Witches are adept at hiding their numbers and no one has ever seen more than a handful of them together at one time."

"We've won a few rock throwing contests since the war, but they have yet to win a single Sparkling contest. We have always had more brio and been more comely than those poor dears — but don't repeat that to any of them, please." Gertrude patted Rachel's knee.

"Lower Mountain Witches do tend to sparkle brighter," Eustice said softly.

Rachel looked puzzled, so Gertrude-Witch spoke, "I will start from the beginning. Over a thousand years ago in the days of our great-great grandmothers, things were not as they are today. Lower and Upper Mountain Witch Kingdoms had little to do with each other. Oh, sometimes we did trade with them. They would leave objects for us on the path leading up to their Big Rock Mountain, and if we liked, we put an item of our own next to theirs. If the trade was accepted, the next day, our item was gone and we were free to take their item in trade. They had their place in the Big Rock Mountain, and we had ours in the foothills and plains. Then one day, two witches – one of theirs and one of ours – were out by the river looking for pretties. Both went for the same one at the same time. Neither would yield and Petra Witch grabbed the Upper Mountain Witch's hair and pulled it. That was the start of the Great Mountain Witch War. The Upper Mountain Witch screamed for help from her sisters, and, they being closer, arrived in force and released the Upper Mountain Witch's braids from Petra's grasp. They then made off with the pretty.

"That would have been the end of it, but they then blocked our access to the paths leading to the quarries where the best pretties could be found. Queen Lucinda organized a party of the most Sparkling Mountain Witches, and they removed the obstruction from the path and carted away barrel after barrel of stones. The next day, our village was raided in retaliation by the forces of Queen Alarica the Brave of the Upper Mountain Witches and my great-great grandmother's sewing machine was taken away by the raiders. From that point forward it was open warfare between our two kingdoms. They built damns to block the streams we needed for our villages. Since these damns were so high up in the mountains, we had to enter far into their territory to reach and destroy them.

"They had the advantage as they were able to use their great skill at rock throwing to force the retreat of our people. They would hide behind trees and boulders and ambush us as we came up their mountain.

The Upper Mountain Witches used their rock throwing skills to such effect that when Juliette-Witch, one of our sisters, chided the Upper Mountain Witches from the valley, even to the point of turning, raising her skirt and mooning them, thinking she could not be hit at such a range, she had taken a large pebble right between her eyes and fallen straightaway onto the forest floor where she remained stunned even after help had been summoned and a bucket of water from the river, cooled by the recent snow melt, had been poured over her head.

"Finally, we got smart. We may not be as tall as they, or as good at throwing, but we do sparkle brighter. That we do," Gertrude said, emphasizing the word sparkle. She paused for a moment, then continued, quickly, perhaps worried Eustice might interrupt her again.

"We marshaled our superior numbers and inventiveness and drew the Upper Mountain Witches into open battle where they would be unable to hide behind their boulders and hurl rocks at our forces." Eustice witch nodded at this last, proud of her Lower Mountain Witch sisters' inventiveness.

"We cleared the ground around our village so they could have no cover from which to hurl stones at us then we set up tables in the Village Commons and put the best of our Great Pretties on them. We knew they were watching us from the hills and trees, so we were confident of our trap. Between our cottages we set up teams of witches with nets and waited. The first day and night, nothing, but we knew something was up because even the night sounds we had been hearing since the war began were gone. The woods were silent. They were watching us.

"After three days of nothing, morning broke upon the village. Our lookouts had spotted Upper Mountain Witches creeping about. Lucinda said, 'Dear Witches, today we change history. Today we defend our rights from assaults by the *Lil' Bitches'* - that was the name given to the Upper Mountain Witch raiders."

"Today," Lucinda continued, 'we turn the tide against them. Sisters, prepare your nets."

"Our sisters made ready, and not half an hour later, we heard the Rebel Yell of the Upper Mountain Witches as they descended upon the commons towards the Great Pretties. On the signal, our Witch Artillery Teams fired their nets upon the marauding Upper Mountain Witches.

The 'Battle of the Great Pretties' followed. It was bitter, and it was ugly. Hair pulling, rock throwing, spell casting and even a musket shot here and there. By the end of the morning it became clear that we had the upper hand. Over a dozen Upper Mountain Witches were ensnared in our nets and safely ensconced within our cottages. Eventually, a horn sounded –their horns usually brought terror to us – but this time it was a call to retreat and the remaining Upper Mountain Witches fled with their forces in a shamble.

"We anticipated a grave counterattack, for Lucinda, in a moment of foolishness, had ordered the brass cannon loaded with a bound and struggling captive Upper Mountain Witch and fired at the Upper Mountain Witches as they fled. This is still known as the 'The Great Atrocity'. Even we Lower Mountain Witches have to admit that Lucinda had been a real bitch to do that.

"The so mistreated Upper Mountain Witch was horribly singed and out of sorts for the next century, but retaliation was not long in coming. Queen Alarica spoiled our great victory with a midnight raid upon our village and made off with Queen Lucinda. The Upper Mountain Witches then took our, now badly-named Lower Mountain Witch Queen, Lucinda The Lucky, to the top of the highest peak, shaved her hair, stripped her of all her pretties, put her in the bottom of a barrel filled with pine cones and rolled her down the waterfall. That was when the Witches Council had enough of our quarrel and sent Representatives."

"Representatives of the Executive Committee, no less," Eustice added.

Gertrude ignored this interruption and continued. "They declared an immediate cease fire and sent representatives to both Kingdoms and forced the two sides to meet. After days of tense negotiation, our kingdoms hammered out 'The Treaty of Big Rock Mountain'. The terms of the treaty were thus; Petra- Witch had to apologize to Maggie-Witch, the Upper Mountain Witch whose hair she had pulled, the Upper Mountain Witches had to return my great grandmother's sewing machine and Lucinda had to forfeit the brass cannon that was the symbol, at that time, of her office, to the Upper Mountain Witches, and relinquish the title 'The Lucky' in recompense to the Upper Mountain Witches for their burned sister. The Upper Mountain Witches also had to remove the damns on the streams and allow us access to the quarries, and formal arrangements for diplomacy and interaction agreed upon and maintained between the two kingdoms," Gertrude ended.

That war must have been some cat fight, Rachel thought.

Chapter 23

Eric squatted and used the rock behind him to lean his backpack against. He had made it up the ridge before his father - but just barely. He could hear, but not yet see his father. In a moment, Dan would be making the turn onto the summit.

"I am now officially out of shape." Dan, panting, collapsed next to Eric.

This gave Eric some satisfaction. Wasn't his father the one who hit the gym religiously, at least before the move and new job?

"Let's take fifteen and rehydrate," his father said.

Eric nodded. From their vantage point, they could see the valley below with its rows of evergreens. A hawk flew overhead. Dan took the folding map from out of his front pocket and studied the area while Eric rested.

"The river widens about half a mile down the ridge." Dan pointed behind them. "We can find a safe spot to refill our canteens and have water for cooking tonight. It looks like a good place to set up camp."

So, they weren't going into the valley today, Eric thought, for the river was in the other direction.

"This sure is a beautiful site," his father said.

"Yes, so peaceful. Hard to believe we are only six or seven miles from the freeway."

An hour later they made it to the river. This time his father arrived first. Pacing himself, Eric thought, that's why I'm wasted and he's not. He let his father choose the place to set their tent. The site was elevated above the bank, but still near enough to the river for quick trips. The view of the riverbank, the tree branches overhead, the stones lying by the shore, and the rhythmic movement of the current created a pleasant environment for a camp.

After putting up their tent and starting a fire, Eric explored around the camp. "Hey, Dad, look at this!" He held up a melted stone. It was collapsed in the center forming a bowl shape.

"Now this is strange," his father remarked.

"Maybe someone put it in their campfire," Eric said.

"No. The melting point of rock is between six hundred and twelve hundred degrees Celsius. That is far hotter than a campfire would get." Dan took the rock from Eric and turned it over in his palms. "This really is strange. I wonder what could have done this?"

"Could it be something pre-historic?" Eric asked.

Dan sniffed the rock. "No, it smells like it burned not too long ago." He put the piece into his pack. "I think I'll take this back with us and ask around at work."

***

Towards early afternoon, mountain witches from throughout the realm started arriving into the village. Some walked, but Rachel was intrigued to see dozens come on the back of 1920's and 1930's style pickup trucks - shiny black models with free-standing headlights, chrome framed grills, and wooden railings on the beds – similar to those she saw in the 1940 film, "The Grapes of Wrath".

Like small children, disembarking from their buses at the start of summer camp, the mountain witches flooded out of their vehicles en masse. They didn't run, but moved rapidly in their bounding style. Most carried wrapped presents. Rachel shuffled where she stood, uncomfortable to think these may be for her.

After all the vehicles were emptied of their inhabitants, a white carriage with gold trim, of the type seen in movies set at Versailles in pre-Revolutionary France, pulled into the yard. Rachel ran forward to take a look at the piece. Snouts of dogs stuck out the passenger windows. As if spring loaded, the door snapped open and steps dropped down one at a time like a slinky. Out came a mountain witch with a dog at her side. Rachel could not tell the breed, but it looked expensive, like a show dog. Two more witches, likewise accompanied by dogs of the same type, but different colors, came out.

For the next five minutes, Rachel watched, transfixed, as witch after witch, all with dogs at their sides, exited the carriage. There had to be nearly thirty pairs. There was no conceivable natural way that the vehicle could have held more than a small fraction of the dogs and witches that disembarked. Rachel had seen many strange things over the past months, but this was the most incredible. She still wasn't convinced her time with Katie that night in her camp had not been a dream.

Gertrude Witch spent the next hour introducing her. There were the mountain witches from the village across the valley, mountain witches from the other side of the realm and their "partners" as they called them, domestic animals; dogs, cats and wild ones; raccoons, beavers, bobcats, weasels and enough other types of creatures to do a respectable job of filling Noah's Ark. There were even witches from Erzsebet's village whom Rachel had not yet met, as well as a handful of Upper Mountain witches. One of them had a fox by its side and when the witch introduced it, the creature bowed with a flourish, staring up at Rachel with intelligent, amber eyes. By this time, Rachel, now at the point of sensory overload, could only return the bow and mutter a polite greeting.

When Agnes mentioned needing more water for the kitchen, Rachel immediately volunteered to go to the river to fill a pail. The air away from the village was refreshing, and as she entered the path, the dust stirred up by the morning's activity dissipated.

She reached the river and dipped the bucket in. On the surface of the water, she saw the reflections of the sky, the trees, the rocks and Katie. Katie? Rachel jumped back, for on a rock on the opposite side of the small cove, stood Katie, in her little yellow dress, watching her.

Chapter 24

I teach you the overman. Man is something that shall be overcome. What have you done to overcome him? ... All beings so far have created something beyond themselves; and do you want to be the ebb of this great flood, and even go back to the beasts rather than overcome man? What is ape to man? A laughing stock or painful embarrassment. And man shall be that to overman: a laughingstock or painful embarrassment. You have made your way from worm to man, and much in you is still worm. Once you were apes, and even now, too, man is more ape than any ape.... The overman is the meaning of the earth. Let your will say: the overman shall be the meaning of the earth.... Man is a rope, tied between beast and overman—a rope over an abyss ... what is great in man is that he is a bridge and not an end."

Friedrich Nietzsche

"What are you doing here?" Rachel stared at the sorceress.

"How are you, Rachel?" Katie asked.

"I'm good," Rachel answered, reflexively, and let the bucket fall to the ground, the water soaking her shoes.

"Don't be afraid. I'm still your little friend. You are not happy to see me?"

"No. I don't think so." Rachel backed away from the river. "You lied to me."

"I never said I was a mountain witch."

"You led me to believe so." If Katie had not meant to deceive her, why would she know what Rachel was talking about?

"I am part mountain witch, if that satisfies you."

"You're a sorceress!"

"You say that as if it were a bad thing."

"What is it, then?"

"It is a bit like being a witch, but they work by intuition and custom, while we go much further. We study mathematics and the principles of the Cosmos, and apply this understanding to the Power."

"So, you're just a powerful witch, then? A super witch?"

"No, not that either. Our power comes from outside ourselves, whereas yours comes from within. That is a simplification, and not quite accurate, but it best describes the difference. We draw upon the power of the Sun, of the Interstellar Plasma, of the heat in water, of the energy in life forms."

"So you are a parasite?"

"Parasite, Rachel? All life draws energy of some sort from its surroundings. You draw power from the Earth as you walk, from the water as you swim, from the life around you. The only difference is that you store power within yourself and draw your power from the Earth without being conscious of it. When I draw power from the Earth or Sun, or water, I use the power directly from its source; I channel it to the task at hand. It never truly enters into me." She waved her hand as if conducting an orchestra. "Think of us as conductors, witches as the players."

"How does that make you so different?"

"Because my power has no theoretical limits. As much power as I take hold of, I can channel. It does not need my body as a medium. This amount of power would burn you out if you drew it into yourself, although your natural capacity does exceed that of most witches."

"How do you do this?"

"It is a combination of natural ability, for we do have a small percentage of witch in our makeup, and a study of the laws of the universe, mathematics, and what you call physics – although my kind does not recognize the distinction in disciplines. To us physics and mathematics are the same."

"So, I could do this?"

"No. You have to be born with the potential and you are too much witch to be a true sorceress. Born, or rather, reborn. I lived a mortal life first. A very short one of which I have little recollection. So shall you be reborn, if you follow me. That is how I am part mountain witch; we have the same genesis – an earthly human life followed by rebirth into this world here. But I can show you things, teach you things, these mountain witches cannot."

"So why do the Sisters think you are up to no good?"

"Because our intentions are different. They want you in their stable and under their control. That is why they are being so kind and solicitous towards you. I am not their only foe, and I'm sure they have at least half-an-eye on your potential military value." Katie eyed Rachel like an adult speaking to a confused and wayward child. "I seek no limit to my potential. No limit to exploration and discovery. This makes others uncomfortable. Strength and freedom frightens people, Rachel, witches not excepted."

"But, Katie, I have a hard time believing my sisters are so narrow-minded as that." Rachel looked down at the water.

"Rachel. Man, and I am including witches in this category, is simply a bridge, a transitory state in the evolution of intelligence." Katie widened her arms, palms facing Rachel, fingertips to the sky. "Look around you. How many are truly interested in fulfilling their full, unlimited potential? How many even wonder what that potential might be? Your parents and their friends, tied as they are by Bronze Age superstitions? And the mountain witches? They are cute little creatures who cannot see beyond their own society. True, they have some power, but they use it in petty ways."

"They are kind and gentle!" Rachel shifted her weight.

"I have not said they aren't, Rachel, but you are different. I saw this in you. You study. You wish to learn and are not content with what others tell you. That is why I let you explore yourself rather than spoon feed you. On your own, you have learned so much – you need only a key to open it. I can be that key for you."

"How?"

"Come with me and I will show you."

"I can't leave my sisters. This is the first place I have ever been happy," Rachel said. "They are so kind, and their village is so beautiful. Katie, you should see some of the things they make. The craftsmanship is out of this world."

"Moissanite? I can show you a planet made of actual diamond. I will bring you to it, and you can tear off as large a chunk as you wish -"

"I have to go." Rachel fumbled for the pail. "I have to go."

"I will be around. Think about what I have said." Katie waved goodbye, hopped off her rock and disappeared into the brush.

Rachel re-filled the pail. If more water was needed, she would bring Gertrude or another friend with her, perhaps even Karen and Jakob — even if she had to use a pretext to do so. Katie's appearance at the river had shaken her and she resolved not to allow herself to be caught alone a second time.

On the path, Rachel was met by the mountain lion as she turned the corner. She was close enough to see its fur of yellow and red ochre. Its mouth was closed, but Rachel could imagine the sharp teeth inside. She stopped. The cat stood there for a moment, then sat and looked up at her.

Well, now's as good a time as any to become acquainted, she thought, and walked towards the animal. "Hello."

Rachel offered her hand slowly. Seeing no defensive or aggressive response, she petted the animal, which it allowed – though it did not reciprocate the affection. Sophie followed behind Rachel until she reached the first cottages of the village, then veered off and headed back into the woods.

Chapter 25

When Rachel returned to the village, a craft fair had opened and Millie held a green and red, Christmas colored scarf. Such expert crafters as the Mountain Witches could not help but share their productions with each other. As Rachel passed their tables, several trades were taking place.

Mountain witches, Gertrude had told her, preferred barter to money transactions. When they did require currency, they exchanged moissanite or other raw materials mined from their mountain for credit in the Citadel's bank, or in silver reals, the Citadel's currency. Every decade or so, the Lower Mountain witches debated issuing their own money, but the Upper Mountain witches had no interest in the idea and it never went anywhere. In their view, retaining a subordinate status – both politically and economically - to the Citadel and its Witches Council had its advantages. Rachel could see the logic in The Upper Mountain witches' objection to making their own currency. They preferred informality and did not like to call attention to themselves or their Kingdom. She had also noticed that, while Annalisse appeared to have more authority as a queen than did Queen Erzsebet, Annalisse was rarely addressed verbally as "Queen" and eschewed the courtesies and trappings of office.

In the far end of the village square, the rock throwing contests had begun. Rachel stopped to watch she had only seen a few Upper Mountain witches. Several were gathered, and dressed in brown and gray clothes, they resembled medieval peasants more than Lower Mountain witches. Their sandals had elevated soles made of hardwood and were fastened with cord. Two of the witches had short, page-boy cropped hair. The third had longer hair tied into a ponytail with a piece of twine. Neither looked directly at Rachel, but she considered this, not as unfriendliness, but, rather, simply a manifestation of their private and reticent natures.

After the rock throwing, there would be a musketry competition. The idea of these little women firing ancient black powder weapons piqued her interest.

Queen Annalisse remained coarser of dress and manner than the Lower Mountain Witches. She wore the same outfit she had when guiding Rachel up her mountain. She didn't speak but looked in Rachel's direction. Rachel smiled in recognition. Annalisse did not smile, but returned a nearly imperceptible nod and whispered into the girl's mind, as Katie used to. *Welcome again, child-witch, to this mountain.*

Sophie approached Queen Annalisse and nudged the old mountain witch with her snout. Annalisse patted her on the head and whispered something into the animal's ear.

Rachel stood with Karen while the witches lined up for the Sparkling contest. "How did the sorceress block you from approaching me? I never felt her channel, unless she was working one of her tricks, like playing a CD without a player."

"Katie channeled the Power without it entering, her as it would a witch. It is not really channeling, not as you know it. Also, different strands of power are used," Karen answered.

"What about our trip through the stars. Is that what she wants? To use my power to travel?" Rachel had eventually told Gertrude and Eustice about this, after initially withholding it.

"She bonded with you so she could evaluate your strength. Simple travel is not a problem for her as she can make herself effectively massless. What she did with you was probably a trial run for something greater"

"What?"

"That is why we are here. To find out and to protect you."

As Gertrude would say, the mountain witches were all sparkling, dressed in their finest colors. Most wore hats and bonnets and many had on multi-colored aprons. One witch brought a live mink to wear as a shawl. "Can't use that!" the other witches cried. The thusly chastened witch set the creature down and said, "Stay here, Hermann. I'll be done by and by."

A single upper mountain witch entered as a contestant, wearing a one-piece dress, burlap in color, and tied at the waist with a belt of rope. Despite the crude outfit, which was more practical for the harder life of the Upper witches, the witch so dressed had an air of dignity. Perhaps because she stood so still and lacked the energetic eagerness of her Lower Mountain Witch contemporaries. Had Queen Annalisse asked her to enter the competition? Despite her short, close-cropped hair and lack of adornment, the witch would have had Rachel's vote.

Witches, with their clipboards passed along the row, examining each contestant in turn. Each witch curtsied to the judges after being examined. When they came to the Upper Mountain witch, she bowed slightly at the waist rather than curtsy as the other contestants.

Rachel couldn't keep from clapping as Eustice bowed. The witch was dressed in her finest dirndl of viridian green skirt, crimson velour apron, and cream bodice, and upon Rachel's insistence, had worn the necklace she had given Rachel as a present.

After all had been examined, poked, and prodded, the judges walked, to the corner of the green and stopped under the mammoth oak tree. Overhead, leaf clusters, green and healthy; acorns and remaining catkins, the white cylindrical flower clusters that bloom in spring, fluttered in the breeze. From the distance, Rachel could watch their animated discussion. Yet, despite the apparent drama in their deliberations – judges gesticulating wildly, several stomping their feet, some clapping their hands – the meeting was short.

To Rachel's surprise, they went, as a group directly to the sole Upper Mountain Witch contestant who stood alone. She was happy for the witch, glad they saw the majesty in the simplicity of that witch's dress and manner. Still, she had hoped for Eustice to win.

Again, to Rachel's surprise, the Upper Mountain witch bowed to the group and walked away, heading in the direction of the Upper Mountain Witch contestants who remained on the green. When she reached Eustice, she stopped in front of the Lower Mountain Witch and kissed her on the hand. The witches gathered around the green exploded in applause.

Eustice had won the "Sparkling" contest. So many witches lined up to congratulate her that it was some time before Rachel was able to see her. Even after witnessing it, Rachel still wasn't quite sure what the contest had been about.

"I am so proud of you, Eustice-Witch," Rachel said when her turn finally came.

"Thank you child-witch," Eustice said. "Here is your necklace back. Wear it with pride." Eustice handed it to Rachel who put it on.

"Upper Mountain Witches always win the rock throwing contest." Rachel heard Eustice say. The Mountain Witch was still beaming after her victory in the contest and carried the moissanite carved prize, which, in a tradition Rachel could not comprehend, was awarded by Queen Annalisse and the Upper Mountain witch who had competed.

Susan, the final contestant in the rock throwing contest, stood up to the plate. The crowd silenced. She scanned the range, letting her gaze fall on one target after another, but she did not yet raise her rock-throwing arm. Suddenly, in a blur, she crouched, bolted upright with her knees still bent slightly, and let loose the stone. To Rachel, it looked like a single movement.

The rock flew directly through the center of the ring. The crowd cheered. Queen Erszebet presented the trophy to Susan. It was a sculpture of the oak tree carved of moissanite.

Wooden picnic tables were set out across the meadow. In a concession to their larger guests, each one had full size human chairs at the ends and a small platform on top so the larger guests sitting at each would have their plates at chest level. The arrangement contained two rows forming an L. Along the perimeter was a long table for the dishes, reminding Rachel of illustrations of the first Thanksgiving at Plymouth.

At the edge stood a large pot of honey the witches had collected for Leroy. Beside it lay the carcass of a deer Annalisse had shot for Sophie, which the Upper Mountain witches had carried down the treacherous mountain paths on a sled, two behind pushing, two in front pulling.

Rachel had to move from table to table to avoid offending any of the guests. During each visit, she made new friends. At one table sat a witch who was small even by mountain witch standards and spoke with a sing-song accent Rachel could not fully make out.

Around the tables, witches produced fiddles and banjos and commenced playing square dance tunes of the sort common in Appalachia in the last century. Oh, my goodness, Rachel thought, they are going to dance directly on the tables. And like fairies from an old Irish tale, they did so. Swirling aprons and skirts blurred into a column of movement as the tables creaked from the movement. Up and back they moved, like miniature whirling dervishes dressed in vintage peasant dresses.

Out on the green, Rachel danced with Leroy, as Jakob, apparently a man of many talents, played the fiddle and Karen clapped. From her perch on the rock at the edge of the commons, Sophie, satiated from her meal of venison, looked down disdainfully at Leroy, the bear, as he danced with the witches, raised on his hind legs and rocked from side to side. Aapparently, she did not feel he upheld the dignity of wild animals.

Eustice played the piano. Rachel didn't know why, but she thought her playing this major instrument had something to do with her having won "The Sparkling" contest . Miniature violins, cellos, harps and flutes came out of their cases and witches started dancing to Prokofiev's "Stone Flower" accompanied by this ad hoc orchestra.

Skirts swished and waved, as feet skipped up and down, propelling the witches forward in the dance. Around the circle they went, until they were joined by a new column that, like the tail of a kite, flowed inward until the circle was increased by dozens of witches. Well, this certainly wasn't what Rachel had read about witches. But then, real witches – or, at least, witches of the kind that Rachel knew – were not pagan, supernatural beings. In fact, hadn't Katie often told her that "supernatural" was a contradiction in terms? Witch and other, irregular phenomena such as sorceresses and magical beings, were within the realm of science; just not the science, or level of science, that humans on Earth were aware of. Oh, certainly there were those who suspected there was more out there, but such investigations usually devolved into junk science or sensationalist, unproven, claims and assumptions.

"We must take Leroy down from his excitement. He has a tendency to get too wound up and start breaking things," Gertrude said to Rachel and walked off towards Eustice and a group of Lower Mountain Witches gathered around the table.

"Time for the Honey Pot!" one of them exclaimed.

"Time for the Honey Pot," the others echoed.

"Make ready sisters!"

Agnes and another sister carried a pot filled with honey onto the green and set it under the large oak. Jakob attached a line to it and threw one end over the largest branch. Gertrude arrived with Leroy, the bear jumping around like a puppy, squealing and rolling in the grass, filled with energy and excitement.

Jakob hauled the pot up with the rope and Leroy desperately snatched for it. Each time the bear came close to grabbing it with his paws or snout, Jakob hauled it higher. Then Leroy would take a step back for another run at it. Jakob would lower it and the contest would renew. After he felt the bear was sufficiently spent, Jakob let Leroy capture the honey pot. The instant Leroy had it in his paws, he dropped on all fours and ran off into the woods carrying his prize. The witches clapped and cheered.

After a banquet of wild turkey, pumpkin pie, and various soups and stews, all of which Rachel was required to taste, some with an enticing salt of the sea taste, others sweet from the maple the witches collected from the trees deep in their forests. Jakob stood and proposed a toast. "To our new and dear friend, Rachel, and to our dear old friends from among the Kingdom of the Mountain Witches." He nodded to Rachel, then to both queens.

Rachel raised her glass with the others. Inside was apple cider brought from the Lower Mountain Witch village Queen Erzsebet had returned from visiting. It was seasoned with a spice Rachel could not recognize, but the taste was pleasant and lingered in her mouth. The only alcohol drunk was from a plum wine Agnes all but forced upon Jakob and Karen, as guests of honor from the Witches' Council and visitors from the Citadel.

After that, the witches presented Rachel with gifts.

Chapter 26

Eustice and Gertrude stayed with Rachel as she
prepared for bed that evening. Her presents
were arranged on the shelf – figures of birds
and other animals carved from moissanite; multi-colored
scarves galore of crimson, viridian, red-rose, ultramarine
blue, and other hues popular among the mountain
witches; several bracelets, some of silver, one of quilted
maple beads, and one of moissanite carvings of
woodland creatures; a blanket; and many other items she
had not yet had time to fully examine. All were of
excellent craftsmanship and would have fetched a high
price in her world – even those items made from
common woods such as oak and maple.

"Do you think Katie could be behind all the things
happening to me? My illness, the scurrying around my
campground at night?" Rachel asked.

"She is a sorceress and they are chess players who always
have a grand strategy. I can't say for certain which is
from Katie or not, but she has targeted you to her own
ends," Gertrude said.

"I don't trust her!" Eustice said.

"Let us be calm about this. Sorceresses are crafty and if we attack this problem with emotion, she will have even more of the upper hand than she already does," Gertrude replied.

"What about the Citadel?"

"They wish to care for and protect you, Rachel. The Citadel is run by the Witches' Council and serves as school, library, and parliament for those within our world," Eustice said.

"Rachel, your world has taught you not to trust, to be wary of those around you, but there are other worlds," Gertrude added. "You have experienced much abuse of authority and power, and that has made you understandably suspicious of it, but authority can be used for good as well."

"I know," Rachel said, but reserved that portion of inner life she kept to herself, the part that didn't really know what she believed.

"You are afraid of being hurt, because you have been hurt so much in life already," Gertrude said.

Rachel didn't answer, but folded her arms into her lap and caressed her ring finger. "And the Grabbers?"

"Power attracts all sorts of creatures. I am not certain Katie is behind their appearance. Your channeling is enough to attract such sorts and as a child-witch they know you are vulnerable to their control," Gertrude said.

"Did Katie make me ill?"

"I would not put it past such a creature as her!" Eustice sped up her knitting, attacking the yarn in effigy of Katie.

"I am not so certain," Gertrude said. "Her actions may have led to your illness, but it may not have been directly caused by her. Travel between realms, between worlds, can also lead to a sickness in those untrained in the use of the Power, and she did signal us, probably knowing she couldn't heal you as we could."

"What about the other missing girls?" Rachel asked.

Gertrude sighed. "We do not know. We believe she may have attempted to bring them into this world and failed. Their power was not sufficient. After that, we don't know. They may have fallen prey to other entities, such as the Grabbers and Possessors. Those two creatures of malevolence often work together."

Rachel went to bed with her mind and feelings in tatters. Eustice stayed up with her, but eventually Rachel pretended to fall asleep so she could be alone with her thoughts and emotions.

So many factions wanted her. Which could she trust? Katie was the most familiar of these, familiar through months of contact, but the mountain witches were the most friendly. The Citadel? She was still wary of them, although both Jakob and Karen had disarming manners and had pulled her out of her mountain camp to safety.

"We are the purpose, you and I. Our lives are ends in themselves. Together we can reach the heights of exploration and achievement," Katie had said.

As in the first night of her illness, her sleep was full of dreams. Katie running across the shelves in Rachel's room, Queen Annalisse appearing from the shadows the morning of their first meeting, Karen watching Rachel from the church parking lot, Jakob walking his dog. The wind whipped the branches where the forest began and the village ended and she could see their shadows moving through the window in Eustice's cottage. As the night reached the Witching Hour of 12:00 a.m., the clouds parted and the landscape became illuminated by the blue-green light of the moon. Rachel gave up trying to sleep soundly and lay in bed, between moments of waking, half-waking and sleep, thinking of Katie, and of the mountain witches, who she now loved.

Something roused her to full waking; a flash – possibly of lightning. But no, there was no storm and the light was cool light, not the warm fire of lightning. Again her room flashed, as if a blue flashbulb had been ignited. Rachel rose from the bed and went to the window. The light flashed again. It came from the forest, in the direction of the stream, where she had encountered

Katie that morning. She quickly dressed, and grabbed her knife from the chest Gertrude had provided her to store her gear. She checked the action of the opening and clipped it to the inside of her front jean's pocket for quick access.

Chapter 27

One must have chaos within oneself, to give birth to a dancing star.

Friedrich Nietzsche,

Thus Spake Zarathustra

R achel entered the forest at the same point where she had gone up the path with Queen Annalisse the day they stalked the wild goat. She passed Leroy collapsed on the forest floor, under an evergreen, honey pot cradled in his paws, snoring peacefully.

Rachel sensed she was not alone, as she made her way through the dark woods, illuminated only by starlight and moonlight, using the blue light as a beacon to guide her, but heard no sound of pursuit. Even those regular sounds of night, the chirping of crickets, the occasional hoot of an owl, the scurrying of small creatures that her days in her valley camp had attuned her to, were absent. She increased her pace. For an instant, she thought she caught a glimpse of a large cat's silhouette reflected in Agnes's cottage window, for that mountain witch's cottage was further back than the others, isolated so she could write her romance novels in peace, but when Rachel turned, she saw no cat. Was her mind playing tricks upon her? She had been surprised early in the day by Sophie, the cougar at the party; possibly her imagination was now seeing the feline in the shadows.

Katie emerged from the ridge, spotlighted by diamond blue light emanating from her hand. "Come girl, I will be your puppet master. Come with me and I will show you things you cannot discover on your own-"

Rachel halted before reaching her, feeling the familiar tug the sorceress held as the first friend Rachel had known when discovering her ability to channel, yet remembering the sorceress's deception as to her true nature. She stared at Katie in the distance. Her little friend could not be all bad – and what if all of this had been an elaborate deception by the Blue Dress People to gain Rachel's trust so she would willingly go to the Citadel with Jakob and Karen? After all, who was she to all of them, and what had she done for them that they would shower her with presents and attention?

Katie offered a world without responsibility, without aging, without concern; yet these temptations could also bring a lack of attachment, maturity, feeling and growth – attributes that she knew in her heart Katie lacked. Was Rachel willing to exchange what she had with the mountain witches, with Gertrude and Eustice who she now considered her sisters, elder sisters and dear, for a grand adventure with the sorceress?

Yet life with the mountain witches, while long and filled with the vibrancy of life, was still ephemeral, still limited. They could not teach her the fundamentals of the Cosmos – because they did not know them. To return home, to Earth? No. She could not do that: it was death there for her. Katie knew this and had bided her time until Rachel left of her own accord. But had Katie given her that near-fatal illness?

Rachel saw the torches before she heard the villagers coming towards them. Jakob was running ahead with a mountain witch, who must be Annalisse. By her side ran Sophie. As they reached the tree line, those with the torches stopped and formed a line, a barrier, between the forest and the village.

"Katie! Katie, dear! You've won Katie. Katie, dear, you've won," Karen yelled from the distance. "Wait. You can use the girl, just let her stay with us. She will not live if she goes with you. You've won, Katie, you've won!"

There was a crash and flash of fire. Annalisse had fired her musket. The sorceress tumbled off the ridge where she stood and into the dark gully bellow.

"No!" Rachel ran for the ridge. She fell over a stone before reaching the top but her forward momentum carried her down the embankment onto the other side.

Vines, twigs and small stones pricked her. Instinctively, she tucked her head in and crossed her arms to shield herself.

Katie was lying in the ditch. Her dress was singed, her face blackened and she smelled of cordite. Rachel got up, ran, then fell, and skidded down to her. She could see no visible injury on her little friend.

"You need to get out of here. Quick." Rachel pulled Katie up and pushed her towards the slope leading away from the ditch.

"Come with me," Katie said, getting to her feet. "I will not leave her without you."

"Good grief, Katie! You have to go. Annalisse can fire more than one shot, you know."

"I know this." Katie produced a ball of blue flame in her palm.

"Don't hurt my sisters!" Rachel cried "I will not go with you and I will never do anything for you, ever, if you hurt them!"

"This will hold them for a little while." Katie let loose the ball of blue plasma from her fingertips. Chords of flame gathered where the ball hit the ridge and formed a barrier between themselves and their pursuers. "Don't worry, Rachel, I will not hurt them – unless they force me into it," she added.

225

"I'll come," Rachel said, finally, after a moment of silence between them. She knew Katie well enough to know the sorceress would not give up, but would stay and fight for possession of Rachel. This, Rachel could not allow, not allow her new friends to be harmed in a fight, could not allow Katie to possibly be hurt herself, and not allow this Kingdom to be turned into a battleground over her soul. She would go and take her chances with this being.

"Take my hand," Katie said.

Rachel did and felt once more the metallic clasping of a bolt locking their bond. Then came darkness as they left the ground together, as they had that night in the camp, the night that now seemed a lifetime ago.

"I have gone through several child witches to find you, Rachel. You are the first one who has the potential to transcend the limitations of your time and place, the way that I did."

"What happened to the others girls?" Rachel asked.

"That doesn't matter."

"It does to me!"

"I did not harm them, Rachel," Katie replied. "With me, your potential will be limitless. You will be the one person from your world to achieve true mastery of the elements and of space and time. You have the power, and I have the skill. Together, nothing in the Cosmos will be hidden from us, nothing forbidden."

"In what way?" Rachel asked.

"I can teach you how to transcend, to go beyond, the limited ability you have as a human and to see the greater reality all around us. To see it and to use it."

"To what end?"

"We are the end, Rachel, you and I. Life is an end in itself: to make discoveries, to so expand our reach as to make it effectively limitless."

"What about my life? When will we return to my world?"

"You have already left it, Rachel. Irrevocably."

"How?" Rachel asked.

"When I carried you into this one, I had to leave your body behind."

Rachel stared at Katie but did not speak.

"Would you really want to return to where you were, how you were, anyway?" Katie asked.

"But my body? This is my body, right here." Rachel touched her chest with her free arm. "And you just said you wouldn't harm anybody."

"No," Katie said without looking at Rachel, still leading her by the hand. "It is a projection."

"How can it be a projection? Karen said I might be able to return to my world. How can I do that if I'm dead?"

"Rachel, Karen is from the Citadel. They have their own motives and their interests are not necessarily yours. When was the last time you felt ill or had to perform bodily functions, aside from breathing, and the occasional meal, which you use to draw power from, but not sustenance?"

Rachel considered a moment and didn't answer, knowing Katie spoke the truth in this. She *didn't* have to breathe. No trips to the bathroom, either.

"Don't worry, I will show you how to create any body you want! The original is the easiest, though. But you can be anything. Want to be Joan Collins?"

"Who is Joan Collins?"

"A bit before your time, maybe. Just leave it to say you can be anything you want with me. Beautiful, but you are already beautiful."

"You mean you killed me when you brought me over?"

"No. Are you dead? You're talking to me, aren't you? I went through the same thing and I am here. You are

more alive now than you have ever been and I did this
for you."

Chapter 28

"Dad! I see something down there. A camp or something," Dan's son called from the ridge.

"I'll be there in a sec." Eric's father finished tying his bootlace, then caught up to his son. Dan looked down at the partially collapsed tent Eric pointed to. The outer fly was covered with dust and leaves and did not look maintained. He took his binoculars and focused on the tent. Atop a large rock near the front of the tent, he saw a camping utensil set identical to the ones he and his son carried. Lying by the rock was a large hardback – a reference manual or textbook, its pages spread open and flapping in the wind. Something in his heart told him this scene was the site of a tragedy. The weather had changed abruptly and the person could have fallen on the slippery ground and been injured. Also, mountain lions still roamed these hills, along with bears and packs of coyotes, and he didn't like to think of the possibility of a perhaps fatal animal attack on the camper or campers below.

"Wait up here son, I'll go down." Dan handed his son a line. "Hook this around that tree, as close to the base as possible."

He started towards the boulder. He could try to climb it, but knew he was nearly certain to slip on its wet, moss-covered surface. Dan cursed himself for not bringing more climbing gear; would it have been so hard to have put in climbing shoes instead of the extra novel he hadn't even read once while out here? Well, he would just have to be extra careful and make sure to have a good hold on the line. Getting back up? He looked across the valley.

"Eric, I can make it down, but getting back up may be more tricky." Dan looked across the valley until his gaze settled upon what looked like an easier way back up. "See that ridge over there? I may have to come back up that way."

"Ok, Dad. Be careful. Please, be careful," Eric said.

"I will," Dan said softly and patted his son on the shoulder. "When I yell *up*, undo the rope. There is not enough for me to make it down with, so I will have to descend in segments. As soon as I find a steady place to tie it, you let it go and I'll fix it to whatever I can. Wait for my signal."

"Will do." Eric looked directly into his father's eyes while answering.

***

...but, when the Rabbit actually took a watch out of its waistcoat-pocket, and looked at it, and then hurried on, Alice started to her feet, for it flashed across her mind that she had never before seen a rabbit with either a waistcoat-pocket, or a watch to take out of it, and burning with curiosity, she ran across the field after it, and was just in time to see it pop down a large rabbit-hole under the hedge.

In another moment down went Alice after it, never once considering how in the world she was to get out again.

Lewis Carroll, Alice's Adventures in Wonderland

Candice decided it was time for another nighttime expedition to the park. Again, she outfitted herself for the elements: boots, jacket, tactical flashlight, and her .38 Smith and Wesson, loaded with the higher velocity, and greater stopping power +P rounds. She didn't expect trouble, but knew it generally came to those who didn't prepare in advance.

She pulled into the service station at the corner from the street where she lived and topped off her tank. And just to be safe, since she didn't know how long she would be outside, went into the convenience store to grab some bottled water to carry with her.

Candice was the only customer in the store and waved hello to the clerk. She came in often and the two had developed a friendly acquaintance.

"Hello, Candice," Tina the clerk said. "Late night out?"

"Not too late, I hope," Candice replied. "I'm tired."

"Same here."

By the time she paid for the drink and pulled onto the street that would take her towards her destination, it was 9:50 p.m. The lights of the businesses and cars reminded her of ships lights and coastline in the distance on a dark night at sea. The odds of finding this Stu person were no greater than on any of her previous trips, but this time she had a foreboding that something would happen.

She touched her revolver; still firmly nestled in its holster. Concealed, but ready for quick deployment. The park would be closed and she would have to leave her car on the shoulder of the road and walk through the front gate. This did not worry her too much, as her detective credentials would get her past any park security. Probably, the only people in the park this time of night would be the homeless, scavenging for any redeemable cans or bottles left during the day. Nevertheless, encountering nighttime predators could not be ruled out.

The river formed a dark ribbon-like line at the edge of the park, almost spooky in its black hole darkness. The only indication it was water were the reflections of light in the distance, closer to the other side. Candice wasn't normally afraid of rivers or lakes, but because she could not see though the dark water, nor where the river's edge started, it gave her an eerie feeling.

A crash came from near the garbage cans. She turned, and heard, but did not see, a creature scurrying away. She shined her light closely. There was no place large enough for a person to hide. It must have been a raccoon, or even a large cat. High up, in the distance was a glowing blue light.

Candice started onto the bridge. What could be the source of that light? Not a law enforcement light flashing; this had more the look of the Aurora Borealis – it was too diffused to be from a single source. Could it be fireflies and a trick of light, an optical illusion? As she made her way across the bridge, she hugged the edge – no sense making herself an easy target.

The bridge was wooden, held up by steel-reinforced beams. Nevertheless, in the silence of the park, Candice could hear it creak under her weight.

Her cell had no signal. Should she go back? No, not yet. Something is going on here. She saw the blue light clearly now, but still could not determine the source.

After jogging several miles past the bridge, deep into the river trail, Candice came to a ravine. She flashed her light into it. At the bottom, she saw pant legs and a white sneaker.

The jeans were light colored and soiled. The jacket hood was pulled. Nevertheless, it was clear to Candice she had probably found one of the missing girls. The girl lay, face down, covered in leaves. She had either fallen or been dragged here. Candice flashed her light up and down the body. Dragged.

The girl's arms were tied behind her back with what appeared to be thin cord or wire. She moved the flashlight up the hood. There was a hole near the base of the skull area. Gunshot, from a small caliber handgun, she surmised, and at close range. The powder burns still showed.

Yet, this park had been scoured – multiple times – by law enforcement as well as local volunteers. Was this a new dump? She looked around for signs of predators disturbing the bodies. Nothing, nor was there the characteristic coppery smell of decomposition one would encounter at such a scene.

Candice had seen her share of bodies over the course of her career in law enforcement, but she shuddered at this find, and had to force herself to breath slowly. In through the nose, filling the diaphragm, then, slowly, out through the mouth. It was a technique a police psychologist had taught her class at the academy, and Candice used it whenever shock or stress overwhelmed her. It worked now and, after several deep breaths, she had cleared her mind and could focus on the crime scene.

What could be the purpose of this? A female serial killer? The only lead had been "ThinkingOfYou" who stated that "she would be wearing a yellow dress" when she met with Kimberly Adams. Going after vulnerable and isolated teenage girls? Was it really a woman? This body was fresh, less than a week dead. Somehow, Candice knew, the other girls' remains were close about.

Candice felt a stir of despair and disappointment. Not that she had expected, truly, to find them still alive, but she was nearing confirmation of the worst. She had to get backup and a forensic team to seal the area. Go back and try to get a signal by the road? That was a forty-five minute hike. Just ahead was a promontory from whose height she might be able to get reception. Forward or back?

She went forward. Ahead, the path winded as it climbed into the hills. At the point where the path narrowed, the view was obscured by haze and fog. The mist was translucent and she could see a bit into it. There were no trees. No silhouettes of trees, yet she had just passed into the tree line and the empty space was behind. Ahead should be forest. Trees and more trees, all the way to Canada, yet there were none. An illusion created by the light and fog? She shined her flashlight at the path, but it simply returned, as if reflected and did not penetrate into the darkness. The blue light continued to flash and Candice pressed on.

As she entered the haze, Candice felt a pulse of power, as if static electricity were discharging into her with every step. Each step became difficult. More like swimming against a current than walking. The mist grew darker and she could barely see the ground at her feet. Her flashlight was useless, worse than useless, as it only reflected back into her eyes.

Candice turned the corner on the path; the fog thinned out, then broke. Ahead, she could see the landscape almost clearly. Gone were the trees and mountain path, with its rocks and damp soil. She was in a field: a treeless field with mountains in the distance. So she was now in a valley? How could this be? Where was she? These mountains were more rounded than those in the Sierras; millennia of wind and rain must have leveled and polished the peaks and crags.

As she passed the final area of haze, the terrain came into sharp focus. It was still dark, as it had been before she entered the mist, but it was later, she could tell. Stars were overhead and the sky was free of clouds. The grass was drier than the ground she had left. In the distance flickering lights were moving down the nearest mountain. The lights moved up and down as if following a path, and Candice realized they were torches. Torches meant people; people who were headed in her direction. She checked for her revolver. It was gone. How could she have dropped it?

At the base of the first hill, she saw a number of small structures. Cottages? A village? There was movement within it, running children – many now carrying torches.

She jogged towards the structures. A hundred meters, or so, before Candice entered the center of the village, several little girls emerged from the dark. One appeared to be carrying a rifle. The other two held items, rocks perhaps, clenched tightly into each fist. Were they afraid she was going to harm them?

"Hello," Candice called to them and held her hands up in the universal gesture meaning I am unarmed and I mean no harm. They stopped. The one in the center slung her rifle over her shoulder and advanced towards Candice, who interpreted this action as meaning they did not fear her or mean her harm.

The girl stopped several paces in front of Candice, close enough for the detective to see that this was no child. "I opened the gate between our two worlds and I have been waiting for you, Candice Strong," Queen Annalisse of the Upper Mountain Witches said.

Chapter 29

Charlie carried his laptop open in front of him, with GPS tracking software running, as the team searched the area where Candice was last known to have been. Candice had left her cell phone on and they had a GPS fix upon its location. They had found her abandoned car and now a team had located at least two bodies and maybe more in a ravine where the path forked towards the mountains. She had to have found this first, Charlie knew, as the GPS software led him directly to the foot of the ravine where he plucked Candice's phone from the bushes. He looked around for any sign of a struggle. He could see nothing that indicated fight or pursuit. The trees and brush were undisturbed except on the path they had taken down to retrieve the bodies. Where was she?

Charlie dialed headquarters. "We have a missing officer. Foul play is almost certain. We need a team down here ASAP."

"Candice!" Charlie called. He would have his sidearm out, but the SWAT team members beside him had their assault rifles on the ready. He could manage his laptop better with both arms free and refer to the map of the area on the screen. "There is a turn in the path over there." He motioned to the SWAT team leader. "Beyond that it heads into the mountains."

The SWAT team leader raised his hand to halt his people, and Charlie knew he was wary of a possible ambush where the path twisted and turned. The team huddled around him. He motioned two to leave the path and circle around off-trail to the front of where it turned so they could see what was ahead. Another officer, holding a netbook, pointed to the screen. They had aerial surveillance over the area. It looked clear from the air, but both Charlie and the SWAT team leader knew that only boots on the ground in a direct visual inspection could be sure.

Overhead, the blades of a helicopter whirled. Charlie monitored the radio as he and the team scoured the ground. At the end of the trail, they found Candice's sidearm still in its holster. She would not have abandoned this. Something had happened to her.

***

The descent into the valley camp was more treacherous than Dan expected. At some point there had been a trail, but it was no longer usable. He came to the end of his line before finding a secure place to tie it, so he had to climb back up another twenty feet and secure it on a piece of granite protruding from the side of the bluff. He estimated that would leave him nearly thirty feet untethered at a slope of nearly sixty degrees. Not good, but he had at least avoided the steep drop at the top. If things got rough, he could crawl the rest of the way down.

His clothes were covered in dirt and he was as scraped up as he had ever been in his life, more even than he had been as a child spelunking in the hills behind his parent's home. Finally, he reached the bottom. The tent fabric was to his left. He carefully stood, wiped his dirt caked hands on his pants and called out. "Hello? Hello? Is anybody there?" He called again and waited. There was no response, no stirring from within, no movement or sound. Dan approached the tent.

He slowly turned back the corner of the flap. Inside was a girl, but he made no attempt to rouse her. Her eyes were closed, her head resting on a pocket of her sleeping bag. The face was the utter white of a lily; framed by her black hair, gently falling by its side, as if carefully and gently arranged by death itself. He knew at once it was the missing girl – the one they had met while shopping for a tent.

He vowed that Eric would not see this. No, he would go back up and tell him they had to go for help in the town and, when they were well away from the camp, he would walk ahead and call for help from his satellite phone.

Later that summer, one afternoon after work, Charlie pulled up to the trail Candice had taken months before. He was familiar with it now – he had made the trip dozens of times in his off duty hours – and walked up the trail, following the route she must have taken. He had gone there at all hours, early morning before work, early evening after work, during lunch, and even several times after dark on the assumption that conditions then would then be closest to those when she had disappeared. Was he missing something?

They pulled a total of four bodies out of the ravine in the days following Candice's disappearance. All were young girls ranging from twelve to seventeen. Three had their hands bound behind their backs; a single gunshot to the base of the skull. The other had died of, so far, indeterminate causes, but they were treating it as a homicide. With the death of Rachel Stephenson, that made five girls dead. Detective Candice Strong remained missing.

Search and rescue, forensics, teams of officers and policy academy cadets had scoured every square foot of ground in the weeks since she had disappeared. Nothing.

This time, Charlie simply hiked to the area where the path crossed the ravine and sat upon a large rock overlooking the gulf. The early evening turned to twilight and then to night as he sat.

***

Dan walked out onto the deck and sat beside his son. After some minutes, watching the pinks, reds, purples and yellows of the sunset, Eric spoke, "Where do you think she is? I mean, what happened to her, her consciousness? Did it just die and disappear or did it go somewhere?"

His father sighed. "Son, if I knew that, I'd be God."

***

"We were too late with the other four, and now we've lost this one, too," Jakob said.

"No, I don't think so. We managed to teach her enough that, when the time comes, she will leave this sorceress," Karen answered.

"What if she kills Rachel? Like the others?" Candice asked.

"Katie didn't kill the others. When they didn't serve her purpose, weren't powerful enough for her ends, she discarded them. This made them vulnerable to pairs of

Grabbers and Possessors. A Grabber took their power, and a Possessor used a human to kill and dispose of them after they were drained," Karen said.

"I may have an idea about that Possessor. There was a human, a homeless man – Stu – I was searching for. They could have got to him."

"Yes, Candice, we are aware of this man. He was taken against his will and is a victim as well."

"Do you know where I can find him? I am still a police officer, and it is my duty to locate him and protect him."

"I am sorry, Candice, but we had no choice but to end this creature. The Possessors destroyed his mind, and we could not save him. I, my sisters, and the Witches' Council have been working for years to bring this sorceress's activities to an end," Karen said.

"What is this purpose of hers you speak of?" Candice asked and looked at Karen.

Karen returned the look, but did not answer. Queen Annalisse came up behind her, Gertrude and Eustice by her side.

"Well, I'm still on the case, and I'm not giving up. I'm going to bring that girl back safe,'" Candice said.

"She is already lost to your world. You must understand that," Jakob said.

"These things weave a thread, Candice," Karen said. "A sort of quantum entanglement. The witch under which I was apprenticed as a child, Mary-Beth, began this search nearly forty years ago. There are many interconnections and I will need you to help us puzzle them out. This is why we brought you here. Then we will best be able to help this girl and any others this sorceress may encounter in the future."

"I asked my sisters among the Lower Mountain Witches to present the child-witch with a gift, a necklace, that contains a special gem I may use to track her," Queen Annalisse of the Upper Mountain Witches said.

***

Across the Universe Rachel traveled with Katie.

"First, I will show you a planet, similar to yours, but bigger and of great beauty, unspoiled and unpopulated by hominids. It is where I make my home," Katie said.

Their adventure was just beginning and Rachel knew Queen Annalisse, the mountain witches, Gertrude and Eustice, and the Citadel, with Jakob and Karen, would be searching for them. It would take some time, but she was certain Queen Annalisse and Jakob and Karen, at least, would find her, but for now, she would follow along with Katie and learn what she could, experience all she could, and then, if she still wanted to, make a dash for freedom when the opportunity arose. Her sisters from the Kingdom of the Mountain Witches would be waiting for her.